D· ¨ ·DUE

THE PIER AT JASMINE LAKE

DANIELLE STEWART

D1738918

RANDOM ACTS PUBLISHING

THE PIER AT JASMINE LAKE

Mark Ruiz's life is a structured routine full of well-worn grooves. Board meetings. Dinner with clients. Preparing presentations. Exhaustingly long days strung together over forty-one years of hard work. Retirement is the promise he makes to himself. The item on his list he can't wait to check off.

The problem? Retirement is better in theory than in practice. Three months in he realizes his new phase of life is as stale as the slice of cake they sent home with him on his last day at the office. His newly purchased cabin on Jasmine Lake is supposed to be an oasis of relaxation. The place and time in his life he's longed for. Rocking on the back porch overlooking the lake, he doesn't find peace. Instead, he finds a pervasive kind of boredom he can't seem to shake.

Just as he resigns himself to retirement, Mark receives a letter that could change everything. A glimpse at the life he could have had. But like most things involving family, it's complicated. Dangerously so.

Gwen is faced with yet another dilemma when finding her father means taking on his struggles. With Griff by her side, she will have to decide if not knowing is better than the burden of discovering the truth.

PROLOGUE

Mark

The ice had melted in his glass again.

That was how he kept time now. He'd stopped wearing a watch. The Rolex he'd gotten for his ten-year anniversary at Brand Alliance was sitting in his nightstand gathering dust. There was no longer any point to putting it on every morning. No schedule to keep. Punctuality hardly mattered now.

On a good day, the hours were broken up by arbitrary things. A pitiful to-do list. A phone call he had to make to his utility company. A dentist appointment. A trip to the butcher for the steaks he liked. They would be on sale on Wednesday. If he got there early he could pick the best cuts.

He hardly recognized himself.

Gone were the days of racing from one meeting to the

next, barely having time for a rushed lunch. Terminating an employee, interviewing a potential candidate, team building and business dinners—there had never seemed like enough time. Now he finally understood those older gentlemen in the coffee shops early in the morning. They'd cluster together and chat animatedly about current events or sports. The waitress always knew their names and always had their orders ready before they even sat down. Mark had wondered why they turned up every day at the same place when they clearly had the freedom to do anything they wanted. Now it made sense. Routine was like a drug, and they needed their fix. Maybe he'd be pulling up a chair to that table soon.

Over the years, his calendar brimmed with things to do. His assistant, Jane Strayer, efficiently managed it. She loaded it up hour by hour, the creator of the buzzing alerts on his phone that indicated another block of his life had been filled. It used to stress him to hear that little buzz. How would he have time to dial into that conference call before having to board his flight? The next alert meant he'd have to cancel on that round of golf he'd tried to work in. It was go, go, go.

He missed it. Now he longed for a day that would be exhaustingly busy. He yearned for a morning when someone wanted him in the boardroom to make a decision. He missed others needing his opinion and his business acumen. Suddenly, his biggest responsibility was remembering to put the trash out on Friday mornings. He didn't need a calendar reminder for that.

As he remembered fondly the tight deadlines set by an auditor, his phone rang and he shot up. The wicker chair he was sitting in creaked under his quick motion. He fumbled to answer his cell.

It was Jane.

"Hello?" Mark cleared his throat. He sounded tired and Jane would notice.

"Hey, boss." That was how Jane had always addressed him. She had been with him for over fifteen years and he considered her a friend. He'd watched her celebrate the birth of her two girls, and he enjoyed staying up-to-date on their latest adventures, welcoming them when they'd spend the day in the office with their mom. They were growing into fine young ladies, and that was all thanks to Jane.

Sadly, Mark also had a front row seat to her marriage falling apart. It was messy and he'd offered to step in more than once, either with extra legal counsel or some good old-fashioned threats to her ex. But Jane was always too proud for that. Too determined to deal with it on her own. And she had been right; she came out on top.

As Jane turned forty, Mark watched with pride as she reclaimed her life, all while perfectly managing his. Jane was a force to be reckoned with.

"Hey, Jane, how's it going?" He was careful to project enthusiasm. He didn't want to raise any flags with her. It was probably true, and maybe a little sad, that no one knew him better than Jane. She'd run his calendar, kept his secrets, and protected his career more times than he could count.

"I'm good. I am so sorry to bother you. I know you're supposed to be relaxing. I wouldn't have called if it wasn't important."

Important? Finally. "It's no problem at all. I'm just sitting out by the lake. I've been meaning to check in with you. How's the new job?"

Jane had moved on, assisting another executive in the

office. Mark could picture her pestering the new guy to ensure he'd prepared for his meeting and drank enough water to balance all the coffee he was chugging. For some reason hydration was very important to Jane. Mark even missed that former annoyance.

"It's different." There was an edge to her voice. Something sad and disappointed. He was being petty, but he couldn't ignore the little pleasure he got from knowing she enjoyed working for him more. He fought a smile as she continued.

"Lyle is different than you in a lot of ways. I took our working relationship for granted. You were the best boss. But I'll manage. In this market I'm just glad to have a job."

"I can make a call. Lyle and I go way back. If he's not treating you right, I'll handle it."

"Don't you dare," she said through a smile he could easily picture. "You know me better than that. I'll whip him into shape eventually. It took me a while to train you. He'll come around."

Mark laughed. "You trained me well. Now tell me, what do you need? You said it was important."

"I shouldn't bother you with this." Jane's voice was low and apologetic now. "It's silly and you worked your whole life to be enjoying your retirement. I hate to even ask."

He nearly told her. It was on the tip of his tongue. *Please ask me. Please need something right now. I can't have another day on this damn porch.*

Instead he pushed the drama aside. "Jane, I'm insisting now. I've got lots of years to be retired. It's a marathon, not a sprint."

"I hate asking for help." She groaned and he pictured her tapping her pencil against her desk nervously.

"I know you do, but do it anyway. Really."

"Marisa has a dance performance. She's traveling and staying overnight with a teammate's family. It's about twenty-five minutes north of you. I can't get the time off. I wouldn't have anyone to stay home with Clara. Bill is busy with his new family." She bit out the words angrily. Jane was still single, but her cheating ex had already started playing house with someone else. "I hate the idea of her not having anyone in the audience. I don't want her to know I asked you—"

"Say no more. Email me the details and I'll be there."

"You sure you have time?"

Again he inched closer to telling her how he felt about this new phase of his life, and how miserable it was. But he wouldn't burden her with that. "I'm glad to go. She's a beautiful dancer. I'll make sure she knows you just casually mentioned it and I begged to be there. And it's lilies she likes, right? I'll bring her some."

"Oh, boss, you really are the best. She'll be so surprised. The girls ask about you all the time. I know it probably didn't seem like much to you, but on those days they'd come in the office you treated them like gold with those special lunches and unlimited access to the supply closet for arts and crafts. Remember when Clara made you that card?"

"The one with the very lifelike drawing of me on the front? How could I forget? My ego took quite the hit that day. Are my ears really that big?"

They laughed, the way you do when you know the conversation has to draw to a close. Jane would be in the office right now and her other line would probably start ringing. She still had things to do.

She kept her voice bright and cheery as she said goodbye. "Come to town for lunch someday soon, okay? I know this is probably the last place you want to be, but I'd love to catch up."

This porch is the last place I want to be. The city is calling me. "I sure will."

Before the line disconnected, Mark heard the clamor of the office. A ringing phone. Voices around the water cooler. Even the ding of the elevator. The line cut off suddenly, and he was left with just the peaceful chirping of birds and the rustling of leaves. It was maddening.

Retirement had been anticlimactic. An entire career punctuated by an office party and some parting gifts he had no use for. When he let honesty creep in, he could admit there was grief to it. He was in mourning. Not of his job, but his identity. Mark had always felt like a whole person. Balanced. Confident. But ending his career had been like amputating a part of him. Come to find out, it was the biggest part of him. There wasn't much left now that it was gone.

Even though it was counterintuitive, he missed the things he used to loathe. Thousands of miles logged on airplanes for business travel, cramped in next to a casual traveler eating their homemade tuna and onion sandwich. Dinners alone, bellied up to the restaurant bar in whatever town he was in. Chatting with the other people in the same solo dining situation. Always having the identical conversations. *Where do you hail from? What do you do for work? Married? Any kids?* It had all seemed like a chore. One he longed to be done with.

Now, sitting on his back porch staring out at the lake, he

knew he was in trouble. The lily pads floating serenely on the surface of the water. Croaking frogs and chirping birds. Fresh air and scenic views off in the distance. None of it was creating the peace he'd promised himself. This was what he thought he wanted. It was why he'd worked so hard.

Wasn't it?

Mark had seen the country. Every state, in fact. It had given him perspective most people were not lucky enough to have. He saw possibilities from coast to coast. Somewhere along the way he'd decided California, the place he'd spent most of his life, was still the best place to settle. Proximity to Los Angeles, where his job had been based, was important, but he'd go north. Just far enough to find some peace.

This property, perched on the banks of Jasmine Lake, was perfect. He could get in his car and be back in the city in two hours or hit the beach in just over an hour. There were three golf courses within thirty minutes, and he was close enough to friends that they'd come for a visit but not so close they'd pop in unannounced. Mark had given it all ample thought. So why now, as he sat on the back porch, did he feel as though he'd blown it?

There had been so many options. Over the years, he'd racked up an obscene number of hotel loyalty points. He'd become a platinum member with the biggest rental car company. He had enough clout at the airlines to travel wherever he wanted. Yet here he was in the backyard of his new house watching the ice melt in his untouched drink, tracing the drips of condensation down the side of the glass like they were thoroughbreds at the track. Rest. Relaxation. Peace. It was wholly unsatisfying.

In his professional life there were perks everywhere he

went, like upgrades to first class and free meals in the Executive Club. People called him Mr. Ruiz, and they said it with reverence. They praised his cuff links and his shined shoes and knew he was someone of importance. That kind of upkeep required structure and a schedule. Even that kept him busy.

Meticulously, he'd gotten a haircut every four weeks, and ensured clean edges to his sideburns. Shopping for new clothes was essential, as was keeping them starched and pressed. For Mark, it was never about being wealthy or flashy. It was about being someone people respected, which was a currency that was far more difficult to earn than money, and harder to keep.

He'd lived his life trying to be worthy of that respect, never taking it for granted. Perhaps there was a part of him that felt an urgency to rise from the ashes of poverty and show the world he could succeed. But that wasn't his main motivation. The people mattered to him. From the staff that cleaned the office at night to the CEO. He was surrounded by people, yet not really close to any of them. That was by design. Being close to people complicated things. He didn't want complicated.

Mark's mother had taught him compassion and how to read a person's need and meet them where they were, rather than insisting they rise up to him. His father, or his father's absence, taught Mark the danger of disappointing people, which was something he avoided at all costs. If you became everything to someone, it meant your absence could destroy them. He refused to weaponize himself and be the detonator that blew up someone else's heart.

Some therapy and life lessons made Mark self-aware

enough to realize that whether through nature or nurture, he had elements of his father in him. Dangerous traits. Ambition mixed with restlessness, a cocktail that made healthy relationships impossible.

In business, a nonstop pace was called perseverance or determination. Those labels left out the reality. It brushed over the fact that people were always left in his rearview mirror as he chased the lightning in the sky. Chronically dissatisfied by his station in life and harboring grand ideas of what he should accomplish, by the time he and his partners were toasting his latest success he was already moving on to the next challenge he'd face. For Mark, it barely registered that he'd accomplished anything at all. There was no filling that tank in him.

Loving that kind of man was impossible. Remarkable women, strong and kind, had tried. His regret was letting them try at all. Starting something more serious, even when he knew better, was wrong. His mentality, the tiny seeds his father had planted, made him indelicate at times. He could be blind to the emotions of the people closest to him, and deaf to their pleas for more of a connection. It's not that he was callous or unfeeling—there was no malice in his heart toward anyone. Mark just couldn't give them all they needed.

Early on, when a relationship dissolved or imploded, he ached. Grieved. These days he knew better. He didn't keep those boundaries up for his sake but for theirs.

The energy he could have spent trying to make the impossible possible, he instead channeled into work. Into climbing rung by rung up the ladder. What no one told him was how different life would be when he finally stepped off at the top. Being a traveling executive meant status. Being unmarried meant freedom. So many of his colleagues groaned and complained about their obligations at home and spent their frequent flyer miles giving their kids trips back and forth from college. Instead of exotic beaches, their perks were spent on family vacations at the big theme parks. Mark would smile as they showed off the pictures and nod at the stories. Yet he couldn't relate.

Family was a foreign language he never bothered to learn. His mother died of heart failure when she was younger than he was now. She never had the benefit of a true retirement even after he began taking care of her financially. She worked more hours in her short life than anyone he'd ever known. Hard jobs. The kind no one else wanted to do. Mark was certain it had shaved years off her life.

His siblings had scattered like pollen in a summer breeze, married and moved as soon as the first opportunity to do so arose. In his opinion they'd settled. But who was he to judge them? Their marriages had survived all these years. They were never alone. His two nephews, now in college, seemed well-adjusted.

Mark treated the act of keeping in touch with them like a business transaction. He focused on what was most important without spilling too many of his resources into it. He didn't miss a birthday; he'd always had Jane send a card. He called on holidays, even showed up for a few of them. One year, though his sister objected, Mark handed out extravagant gifts. His career was taking off. He had more money than he needed. His mother was gone. His siblings were managing their own lives. There was no one left to take care of, so he spoiled them to make up for the time he hadn't spent visiting.

He thought back on his career and realized that was how

it had started. Why it had started. The overwhelming determination to make sure his mother could stop working and be taken care of. Eventually he made that possible, but by then she was too ill to really enjoy it.

As soon as he was able, without fail, he would send his mother a check that would more than cover her expenses every month. Mark ignored her objections. And when she'd finally resigned herself to accepting his help, she would ask him to deliver it in person next time so they could have a meal together. It was a dance they did.

He'd promise he would try, then after breaking that promise he'd have Jane mail the check. It was better that way. If he started to visit his mother frequently, she'd grow to expect it. Plan for it. Then, inevitably, work would ramp up and he'd have to call and cancel. He could practically picture her in the kitchen making his favorite foods when he bailed on her, a hand on her tired back and her hair pinned up away from her forehead, damp with sweat. What would she do with all those tamales? The idea of her disappointment or sadness being his fault was too much. It was better instead to just surprise her occasionally.

Mark eyed his glass of watered-down lemonade and groaned. Mitch and Gary were out of town with their wives, so there would be no afternoon of golf. He could go to the driving range and hit a bucket of balls, but he'd done that the day before.

The letter on the table next to him flapped as the breeze off the lake picked up. He'd tried to forget it was there, regretting ever opening it in the first place. But now, there was nothing to distract him from it.

Lifting his drink off the corner of the paper, Mark held it

in his hand and considered the implications. The damp ring left in the corner from his glass blurred a few of the hand-written words. But he'd read it enough times to commit most of it to memory anyway.

This could be what he needed. Facing the past head-on would surely not be boring. At least he'd be doing something. Golf with his buddies could only fill so much time. Hitting up Vegas and playing blackjack all night was costing him a fortune. The trip he had planned to Africa was still months away. Maybe this letter was a sign from the universe. It was time to finally confront the thing he'd been avoiding. Nothing was stopping him now. He certainly had the time.

But then, impulsively, Mark closed his fist over the paper and crumpled it to a ball. He tossed it into the fire pit at his feet. He'd burn it later. The universe was not signaling him. If he was bored, he needed a new hobby, not a one-way ticket to the past. There was nothing good there.

His past wasn't the attic in his childhood home. It wouldn't be filled with forgotten treasures and nostalgia. Just cobwebs and dust. Instead he could learn chess. Join a book club. Start playing cards once a week. Anything else.

The familiar restlessness he'd battled his whole life began nipping at his heels again. Aching like a blister rubbed raw.

Taking the lemonade in his hand, he drank it down. The sting of the vodka he'd mixed in tingled down his throat. Pulling his arm back, he launched the glass out against the rocks at the lakeshore. It smashed with a thoroughly satisfying sound.

The ice wouldn't melt in his glass again.

CHAPTER ONE

Gwen

Gwen ran her finger mindlessly across the long wooden shelf. The options were overwhelming. It was crammed from end to end with shiny bottles of nail polish. Mismatched in size, they made up a rainbow with endless hues. Normally the treat of a pedicure would have Gwen excited. She valued time with her mother to chat and catch up. But today felt different, rushed and overshadowed.

Indecisive about what to pick, Gwen stood to the side. She opted to let her mother, looming impatiently behind her, select the perfect shade. It turned out a polish called *Sing the Blues* was what she needed. It was a bright cobalt with a little shimmer and matched her party dress perfectly. And that mattered. At least, it mattered to Millie Fox.

The strong smell of acrylic and flowery soap overtook Gwen's senses as they settled into the pedicure chairs. Their normal launch into some neighborhood gossip or discussion of her brothers didn't happen.

Instead, Millie fidgeted, appraising the already busy nail salon. She'd insisted they get there right when it opened, yet the business had already filled with patrons looking for some pampering.

"I hope we don't have to wait too long," Millie whispered just loud enough for one of the technicians to hear. "We have a party to get to," she continued apologetically.

The party.

That was what had been encroaching at the edges of their normally lighthearted time together. Millie had planned the perfect graduation party, a true labor of love. Over the last two months she'd snipped pictures out of magazines and glued them in her notebook, which was usually reserved for a grocery list. It was covered with ideas and tasks associated with the party plans. It was different in almost every way from their usual family celebrations.

This party would be catered by a local restaurant instead of the normal potluck style the Fox family and their friends were famous for. The yard would be adorned with real decorations from the event planner rather than the usual handmade posters and paper streamers. Balloons would be filled with helium rather than the air from the Fox family lungs and taped to a wall to look like they were floating. It was all very legitimate. Formal.

Bizarre.

. . .

The large white party tent in the back of the Fox house took up most of the yard. Tables with matching cloth covers and coordinating chair cushions had been set up this morning. A flurry of strangers were moving in and out, trying rather transparently to cover up any part of the Fox household and yard that wouldn't be seen as traditionally beautiful, and scrunching their faces up in disappointment when their efforts weren't effective. The wood pile, half toppled over, wasn't going anywhere. The old rusted furniture on the deck couldn't be painted in time.

They did the best they could with what they had. Like a thin coat of paint on an old wall, the imperfections still showed through. Gwen had always loved those imperfections.

When Dave had graduated, the whole family pitched in and bought a banner to hang in the yard. Something printed from the local party store. It wasn't fancy but it had his name on it. They'd strung it up on the tattered wood fence and draped streamers from it.

Then when it was Nick's turn, as a joke, they crossed out Dave's name. With a Sharpie they drew in Nick's name. It looked terrible but hilarious. Gwen had assumed, hoped really, they'd be putting her name on the banner too. Any graduation she'd had before this was celebrated rather quietly. Mostly because everyone knew this one, the big one, would be coming. The time when she accomplished everything academically she'd set out to. But now when she finally felt worthy of the old banner and the Sharpie, a brand new one had been ordered. One that matched the theme of bright blue with shimmering letters. One that cost far too much for a one-day affair.

No matter how many times Gwen insisted it wasn't necessary, Millie persisted. When Gwen argued it was silly to spend that much, she'd been shooed away. It was as if they'd forgotten she was a twenty-six-year-old who'd done her share of graduating before this. The only thing this graduation really meant was she'd finally be working a forty-hour week and getting kicked off her parents' health insurance. So much had happened over the last six months, graduating hardly met the standard of excitement they'd all set lately.

Resigned to the schedule her mother had set for the day, Gwen soaked her feet in the slightly too-hot water and let the bubbles tickle her toes. A pedicure wasn't usually high on her list but Millie insisted. It would look great with the strappy sandals she'd picked out to match her dress. Millie had nearly cried when Gwen asked, "Who wears a dress to a backyard party?" That had been her final protest. Making her mother sad was heartbreaking. It wasn't worth it.

"I have to make sure the caterer remembers to bring condiments for the finger sandwiches. I don't want them slathered ahead of time in mayo and mustard. They get soggy and then no one wants them. I read that somewhere." Millie fiddled with her phone and shut off the massage function on the pedicure chair as if it were too distracting.

Gwen reached over and took her mother's phone. "Mom, this is supposed to be relaxing. You don't need to stress about every detail of the party." It wasn't like her mother to be this frazzled by the tiny specifics of an event. Millie was the first one to remind people it was about who was around your table, not what was on it, that mattered. For some reason, what, suddenly mattered.

With a huff, Millie yanked her phone back. "My

daughter just graduated with her master's degree. The hooding ceremony brought tears to my eyes. I'd like the party we throw to show how proud we are."

Show. Show who?

It was starting to make sense now.

"Oh, I get it." Gwen didn't mean to sound condescending, but it was too late. She had and it didn't go unnoticed by her mother. "I know you're proud of me, Mom. You don't have to show anyone else anything. Just because Leslie and Kerry will be there doesn't mean we have to put on some special party. You didn't have to invite them." There were no rules about how to deal with your biological mother and sister after you find them.

Millie looked instantly wounded, her mouth going slack. "This has nothing to do with them. They extended an invitation to us for Kerry's graduation dinner next week. Of course I was going to invite them to your party."

"There are no rules, Mom. It's not a competition. We don't have to impress them or try to be like them."

Millie pulled her feet out of the soapy water and spun to the side. Grabbing her purse and sandals, she stormed off, sudsy footprints in her wake. By the time she reached the door Gwen could see she was crying.

"Damn."

The woman who was about to start doing Gwen's pedicure wheeled her chair over and gestured for the polish she was clutching tightly.

"I have to go get my mom," Gwen apologized. "I'll be right back."

"She got the floor all wet," the owner scolded, rounding the front desk with a towel in her hand. She gestured at

Gwen with a threatening finger. "You have to sit back down. Your feet are wet."

Gwen shook her head and followed her mother's path. "My mom just left. I need to go talk to her."

"You need to sit down or you need to leave."

Gwen slipped, her soaking feet slick on the linoleum floor. She dropped her sandals to the floor and slid them on. "Sorry."

The woman snapped the towel to the floor and glared at Gwen. "Crazy women. Don't come back."

Millie was already in the car, dabbing her nose with a tissue. Gwen made a move for the passenger door but it was locked.

"It's hard for me to talk to you right now," Millie said with a sniffle. The window was opened just a crack. "That was very mean, what you said."

"I know." Gwen's face crumpled. "I just don't want you to feel any pressure."

"The party is for you. I want you to be excited about it."

"I am excited," Gwen lied. In reality there would be loads of people there she wasn't that eager to see. Old acquaintances of her parents. Some second cousins she had nothing in common with. A few neighbors they weren't that close to. There would be chitchat about school and her new job, but ultimately everyone would want to hear all the gory details of her birth family. The problem? They'd be there too. On display like zoo animals. Fielding awkward questions and at the mercy of people trapped under the same tent as them.

Gwen pulled at the handle again, but it was still locked. As some sort of compromise, Millie lowered the window from one inch to two.

"This isn't easy for me," she reported through the heavy emotion she was fighting.

"I know it's not, Mom." Everyone had been rolling with the punches, but it was impossible to act as though nothing was different. Gwen had brought chaos to their lives. Suddenly they were all navigating a thorny patch, and every now and then someone got caught up or pricked. "Can I please get in the car so we can talk?"

Millie rolled her eyes. It was a silly regression that had crept in lately. She and her mother had been reversing roles. It was more than a little unsettling to have to coach her mother out of a tantrum. But it was fair. Millie had earned some breakdowns. She'd spent so many years not having them, too focused on holding everyone else up. She was tired of being strong, and she was leaning into the pain. The least Gwen could do was be there to hold her up.

When the lock clicked, Gwen quickly opened the door in case her mother changed her mind.

"I'm not trying to show off to them," Millie grumbled. "But maybe I do want to show them how loved you are. Maybe I want to show you too. The Laudons have money. Fancy things. I'm sure we'll see it all at Kerry's party. If you'd have been raised in their house—"

"Stop right there," Gwen insisted, cutting her hand through the air. "I don't have a single ounce of regret that I grew up in your house instead of theirs. They're going through a lot right now with the divorce. Things are rocky with her and her sons. Maybe their house is bigger, but it couldn't possibly compete with the love in our house. No chance."

Millie narrowed her eyes and smirked. "It's not a competition." She parroted Gwen's words back sarcastically.

Is this what it was like for her when I was a teenager?

"Well if it was, we'd be winning. Even without the caterer and the fancy decorations. I love what you planned, but can I ask you for one thing?"

"What?" Millie's eyes were soft around the edges again. Slowly returning to the nurturing maternal state Gwen had always known growing up.

"The banner. The old one. Can we write my name on it and hang it up? Sharpie and all. I've been waiting a long time for that."

Millie huffed, channeling a moody tween. "It looks ridiculous."

"We're ridiculous. That's what makes the Fox family so special. Things like that make us who we are. I don't want that to change. Not for anyone or anything."

"Everything is changing." Millie drew in a deep breath. "Nick is moving away for work. You're moving into the house."

"And you're moving out." It struck Gwen suddenly how foolish she'd been. She hadn't given enough thought to exactly how hard the culmination of all the change would be on her mother. Add in the unexpected introduction of maternal competition. One of her sons moving farther away. And the hardest of all, Millie was moving out of the house she'd spent most of her adult life in.

The small condo they'd be moving into was cute with a great sense of community. Their new life would have Bingo nights and shopping trips. It would be the best thing for her father's mobility as he managed his bad back. But had anyone thought how it would affect Millie? Did anyone ever think about Millie?

"It's a lot," Millie admitted, patting the tissue to her nose. "This will be the last party I throw. All of your and your brothers' birthday parties. All the Christmases. The Easter gatherings. It's the end of an era."

"No, it won't be. You'll be entertaining plenty of people at your new place. And you know I can't host anything. I just assumed you and Dad would come do all the holidays at the house. I can't make a turkey. I don't even make good turkey sandwiches. This isn't the last anything for you."

"That's true." Millie smiled. "You really don't know how to do much around the house. Practically useless in the kitchen."

Gwen smiled. "Exactly."

"Maybe your dad and I could come by once a week for dinner and I could show you how to do a couple of things. I have loads of our family recipes. It could be a nice little thing we do."

Gwen wanted to give a resounding yes. Of course she'd like to see her parents. But it had been a long time since they'd been in her life with such frequency. Not since she left for college many years ago. Millie was right, all of this was a lot. Gwen refused to make it any harder for her mother. "Of course, Mom. That sounds really good."

"And then you can cook a proper meal for Griff." Millie straightened up in her seat and her flawless face lit with a smug smile.

Gwen gulped and felt her mother's eyes on her. "You know he's in Boston now."

"Yes. That's basically another continent. No one ever

commutes from Boston to Connecticut. Unheard of. He'd be a real pioneer if he came for the weekends. Practically riding the Mayflower on that journey."

"It's not just the commute." Gwen felt her cheeks grow hot. She'd been avoiding this topic.

"Obviously it's not just the commute. So what's going on with you two? You were all hot and bothered with each other around Christmas. And then even when you met Leslie things were still going strong. He was right there."

"Mom, people don't say they are *hot and bothered* with each other. That's gross."

"Don't deflect."

"I told you what happened with Griff." She had brushed over the topic briefly right after it happened. She was trapped now. Her mother wouldn't settle for that this time.

"Tell me what really happened."

"We were running on adrenaline. This whole search for my birth family was intense. He was avoiding his life. I was trying to sort mine out. We were something familiar to each other. But then reality set in."

"And you chickened out on California?"

"You've been waiting a while to ask me this, haven't you?" She glared at her mother. "It must have been killing you to not know."

"I was trying to let you finish school and start the move back here before I decided to pry. I didn't want to come on too strong and scare you away from being my neighbor."

"My boxes are still back at my apartment."

"Yes," Millie conceded, "but your lease is up tomorrow and a new tenant is already scheduled to move in. I think I'm safe to bother you now."

Gwen knit her brows together. "How do you know all that?"

"Is that really important right now? I'm busy trying to forgive you for sassing me in there all while trying to help fix things with you and Griff. It's a lot of work. Now tell me, what happened to California?"

Gwen leaned her head back against the car seat and sighed in defeat. "It didn't make logistical sense to go to California. Leslie gave me only a name."

"Mark Ruiz." Millie said his name as though the words had been haunting her since she first heard them. Her infallible mother was undeniably human these days. The thought of Gwen's biological father was equally unsettling as the idea of a biological mother had been.

"It's a pretty common name. There were hundreds living in California. Leslie didn't have any more information to help narrow it down. Once Griff and I talked more about it, we both realized we'd be going out there just to put off our lives. But we agreed if anything else came up that would help us find him, we'd do it together."

"And then you ripped his heart out and stomped on it like a drunk tap dancer?" Millie stomped her still bare feet playfully.

"I didn't. Griff was in complete agreement."

Millie tipped her head back. "Oh, the things we tell ourselves to feel better. That boy is crazy about you. And I know my daughter well enough to know you feel the same. You two are wasting precious time. It's foolish. Trust me."

"Trust you? You're the one running out of a nail salon without your shoes on."

Millie tipped her head to the side and sighed. "Griff looks

at you the exact same way your father looked at me the first six times he proposed."

The news struck Gwen like a punch line. Somehow too funny to be true. "Dad proposed six times?"

"Nine times." Millie looked proud of the fact.

"You kept turning him down? I never knew that."

"Kids never know these things. They don't bother asking. They can't imagine their parents were young and in love."

"Can we go back to the part where you made Dad propose nine times? Why? You didn't want to marry him?"

"I didn't want to marry anyone." Millie looked suddenly mischievous as the corners of her mouth curled into a smile. "Or I didn't think I wanted to. I had a string of cruddy boyfriends and I had written men off. In my opinion they were all dogs. Your father was determined to show me he was different."

"They all say they're different."

"They really do. And I knew that. So I held my ground. He and I dated exclusively. I met his family. He met mine. But I didn't think marriage was for me."

"He just wore you down?" Her parents were so in love. Gwen couldn't imagine her father having to chase his mother's love.

"No," Millie corrected. "He didn't wear me down. He won me over. It wasn't like all nine times he just got on one knee and shoved a ring in my face. That was only the first two times. The rest, he got creative."

"I can't picture Dad like that. Big romantic gestures?"

"Not exactly. Thoughtful gestures. He listened. He paid attention. It was refreshing."

"So what made the ninth proposal different? He did

something you just couldn't say no to?" Gwen leaned in. Listening attentively. Her mother was right; she never really imagined her parents as young. In love. Conflicted. They were just together. Always in her mind. She assumed her father bought a ring, took a knee, and asked. Nothing more complicated then that.

Millie chuckled. "The ninth time was different."

"Different how?"

"I was pregnant. We eloped three weeks later. You never noticed how tight the math was between our wedding anniversary and Dave's birthday?"

"Wow." Gwen sat back in her seat and scrutinized her mother's expression. Was she joking? Trying to get a rise out of Gwen? Because it was working. "You should tell me this stuff. I want to hear these kinds of stories."

"I'm telling you now."

This was the kind of morning she had wanted with her mother. "I really am sorry for what I said earlier. I didn't mean to upset you."

"Can you keep that sentiment close to your heart when I tell you something? Just remember how quickly I forgave you."

Gwen braced for another bombshell. The last few months had felt like mortars dropping on her head without warning. "What is it?"

"Griff called this morning. He's coming to the party."

"No, he said he couldn't make it. He had some scheduling conflict he couldn't get out of."

"Apparently you are worth whatever the consequence will be."

"He said he wasn't coming." Her hand flew to her forehead, a cold sweat forming. She wasn't ready to be back in the Fox family house with him. All the questions from her brothers. The teasing. With Kerry and Leslie trying to look comfortable in a sea of strangers. It felt like too much.

Millie reached over and touched her daughter's cheek. "Oh honey, brighten up about it. Who knows, maybe you'll end up back in the tree house tonight."

CHAPTER TWO

Gwen

"You're moving back here? To this house?" Sibyl Meriwether looked displeased by the news. Nearly horrified. The way she turned up her nose couldn't be mistaken. Her large sun hat drooped down as though it, too, wasn't happy to hear Gwen was moving back to her childhood home. "Why would you want to move back into your parents' house? You've just graduated. You could go anywhere."

Gwen felt instinctively defensive. People found it easy to judge the tiny Fox house, dismissing it as too small by today's standards. If her family had any intention of keeping up with the Joneses, they were surely failing. But the Joneses had nothing on the Foxes when it came to the stuff that mattered.

"I love this house." Gwen frowned as she sipped on the fancy punch. It was delightfully bright but sour, looking far better than it tasted. "It's been in my family for generations.

My parents are excited to move into their condo, and I'm happy to keep that tradition alive."

"I know about the condo." Sibyl held a worried expression, as though she were processing dreadful news. "Of course I know they're moving. I just assumed the house would go up for sale. In this market your parents could make a fortune. It's not a big plot of land but it would be enough to build something new on. The school system makes it very desirable. You are all missing out on an opportunity."

It suddenly became clear. *Sibyl Meriwether is a real estate agent.*

"A realtor could make a fortune off that sale too." Gwen shrugged, tipped her head at Sibyl and then made her way to the other side of the yard.

She wondered if people had started to notice. Gwen wasn't sure if it was apparent to everyone in her life. There had been a marked change in her lately. A new confidence. People didn't automatically get to take up her time anymore. They didn't get to say whatever they wanted while she stood there and waited for them to dismiss her. Walking away was an underutilized option, and one Gwen had been embracing lately. Being liked, being polite . . . felt unimportant.

With a steady look around, she appraised the party. *I'm not looking for Griff.* Someone would surely accuse her of that if they noticed her casual glances.

Somehow, even with the upscale details, it was so clearly a Fox shindig. Her heart warmed at how their essence could permeate any attempt to cover up their true nature.

The boys had pulled a bunch of chairs away from the tables and ended up with a circle of rowdy beer drinkers, made up of a few of her cousins and some old high school acquaintances who'd never moved away, telling long forgotten stories of their conquests in the world.

The older crowd, people whose hair was silver or gone, were perched on the benches below one of the old oak trees, looking on with thinly veiled judgment. A few young children had plucked the balloons from their thoughtfully designated spots and had let out the helium. Then blew them back up and began batting them around like volleyballs over the heads of other guests and precariously close to the food. Their little shrieks drowned out the laughing of the boys and the judgmental humming of the elderly.

The spread, which had been artfully laid out, was thoroughly picked over. Gwen imagined it was dismantled in ways the person who arranged it clearly didn't intend for. The trays were all nearly bare. Even the garnishes had been mistaken for appetizers. Someone had taken the nice crystal trays and stacked up the empty ones, making room for a twelve pack of beer. At some point the pantry had been raided and the packaged cookies were out too.

The Fox family and their guests were eaters. The tables were usually loaded with mismatched crock pots filled with chili, meatballs, and BBQ. Everyone's special recipes, signature dishes. You knew Mrs. Welling would bring her coffee cake. Charles from her father's work always brought his famous sausages. Someone could be counted on to bring big bags of soft rolls from the local bakery. They would be torn open and handed out like footballs being passed around. Cans of soda would be dumped into a cooler then slid under the folding table. There'd be one with juice boxes for any little guests. If it were hot, the sprinkler would go on. The muddy yard would make for a fun time. Eventually the adults would end up soaked too, because that's what parties were meant to be. Fun.

This event was a threat to the nostalgia and entertainment, but still they won out. There were big pitchers of punch with tiny glasses. Someone had gone in and gotten a bottle of vodka and big red plastic cups. The dainty finger sandwiches became a challenge. How many could her brothers fit in their mouths at once? The answer was seven, Dave boasting as the reigning champion. After a few more beers someone would challenge him for the title. A good party usually involved the need for the Heimlich maneuver.

Somewhere in the world, Victoria, who was hired to plan this party, was smiling with pride. If she could see how the delicate tapestry she'd created had unraveled, surely the smile would fade. It had only been an hour since the party kicked off and already the Fox family and their guests were dancing on the grave of what she created and they all looked quite pleased about it.

"Leslie and Kerry just pulled in," Millie reported, trying to seem nonchalant as she gestured to her sons. "Put those chairs back where they belong. And how is all the food almost gone?"

Noel was on her, wrapping an arm over her shoulder. "My love, why don't we go open the door for our guests?"

"But—" she looked over her shoulder. "Oh, you guys are something else."

"But we're yours," David called, winking at his mother. Something that seemed to soften her tense posture.

"I'm not ready." Gwen whispered the words to herself, her breath catching in her throat. There would be so many people staring. Waiting to ask questions. What would Leslie think of this odd bunch?

"Not ready for what?" Griff asked, leaning so close to her ear she could feel his warm breath.

She jumped and he steadied her. "Where the hell did you come from?"

"I came in the back gate." He gestured with his chin. "So what are you not ready for?"

A wave of relief flooded her. No matter how much she tried to convince herself Griff wasn't that important, when he showed up, he proved her wrong. "Kerry and Leslie are here. I just feel like we have a bunch of people staring at us, waiting for something to happen."

"Want me to streak across the yard and take the pressure off?" He reached for the top button of his dress shirt and raised a challenging brow at her.

"Keep your clothes on." She jutted a finger in his direction, thumping it to his chest. "It's not that kind of party."

"Not yet."

"You're not helping." She drew in a deep breath. He was helping just by being around.

"You've spent some time with Leslie and Kerry now. It'll be fine."

"My mom is seriously stressed out about having them here. Like the house and the party aren't good enough. It's not like her at all. I feel terrible."

"Oh," Griff said, looking around and nodding. "That makes sense. The big tent. The fancy decorations. Are those little sandwiches? I assumed your dad's meatballs would be in the crockpot. That's why I came."

"Sorry, just fancy little foods we mostly devoured already. Looks like you don't have a reason to stay now."

"Griff," Dave called, waving him over with a beer. "Tell these guys about that time in Texas. That bar that had the horns all over the walls."

"I can run interference for you." Griff waved Dave off. "Your mom loves my jokes."

"Go play with the boys," Gwen said, pushing his chest. "I'll be fine. I'm a big girl."

"Okay." Griff shrugged. "But make some time for me later. I've been meaning to tell you that I know things with us—"

"Later," she promised as he leaned in and kissed her cheek. "But don't be all weird about it."

Griff smiled that cool smile. "You're weird. And congratulations on your graduation. Welcome to the real world. It's pretty awful out here." He strode away and took a chair, pulling it over to the circle the guys had made. Within seconds they'd erupted into laughter. Sometimes she envied how easy it was for men to just be at ease.

"Here's my special girl," Millie called too loudly to seem natural. "Our special girl," she corrected awkwardly. If it were appropriate to plant her face in her palm Gwen would do it now.

Instead, she plastered on a chipper smile and appraised Leslie. There was a heaviness to her shoulders. It was growing worse each time they saw each other, a tired ring around her pretty eyes. She was still beautiful, but she looked worn down like she'd just spilled out of the car after a cross-country road trip. Gwen couldn't help but feel responsible for the changes.

It was still strange to see herself in Leslie and Kerry. Their shared features were unsettling, whereas she'd assumed it would feel comforting. There was so much more to know about these women, yet she could see parts of herself reflecting back. It was spooky.

"Congratulations," Kerry said, smiling brightly. The juxtaposition in their two smiles was clear. Kerry truly was beaming, not an ounce of her happiness forced. Gwen remembered what it was like to be that age. That period of life that was so abundant with possibility. The summer between high school and college. The end of something that had felt endless. The beginning of everything. Freedom just at her fingertips. One last summer to be a kid.

"Congratulation to you too. Glad to be done with high school?" Gwen folded her hands neatly and hung them in front of her body, trying to look relaxed. Glancing over at Millie, she saw the same stance. Nurture and nature were on display in this little circle they were all standing in.

Kerry seemed oblivious to any tension or unease. "So glad to be done with high school. I can't wait to get out to California. College is going to be amazing."

"I heard you are valedictorian. That's a big accomplishment." Millie put a hand on Kerry's shoulder. Gwen watched her mother suck her lip in. She was fighting the urge to match that accomplishment with one about Gwen. *It isn't a competition.* They'd been reminding each other of that jokingly all day.

Leslie patted back the few strands of hair that had escaped her tight bun. "Thank you so much for inviting us, Millie. You have a beautiful house."

"This is the kind of party we need to throw, Mom," Kerry said, looking around in wonderment.

"What do you mean?" Millie asked, her hands fidgeting.

Kerry beamed as she explained. "Everyone actually looks like they're enjoying themselves. Laughing. Like they want to be here. Oh my gosh, those are my favorite. Can I have some of those cookies?"

"The packaged ones?" Noel asked curiously. "Sure. Help yourself. You better get some before the boys decide they're hungry again."

"Speaking of the bottomless pits, you should meet my brothers," Gwen said, looking over to make sure Griff had wrapped up that stupid story he was telling. "They've been really looking forward to meeting you."

"Oh, they're cute," Kerry laughed, her hand coming up to her cheek. "I can say that, right? They're not related to me."

Leslie gave her an annoyed glare. "Kerry Marie, behave yourself. They're far too old for you."

"She's right," Gwen agreed, knitting her brows together. She knew her brothers as smelly jerks who always had something snarky to say. She understood women found them attractive, but she could only see the immature nonsense. "And they're very annoying older brothers. You'll see."

"Well, you know. You have two of them yourself." Noel said.

"They've been jerks lately," Kerry admitted with a sigh.

"They just need time," Leslie insisted, stiffening her back. "It's been a whirlwind."

Again, Gwen couldn't beat back the guilt. She'd been the whirlwind that had swept them all up, demolishing their normal lives.

Millie leaned in and took Leslie's hand in hers. "I was going to offer you some punch, Leslie. But maybe I should just break out the wine?"

Gwen laughed. "Might as well do the punch. Someone spiked it. It's strong."

Millie pointed a finger at her boys. "Seriously? You spiked the punch?" She turned back toward Leslie. "I swear I don't know how they have made it this far in life. They're like little children when they get together. Can't be trusted."

"I'd love some spiked punch," Leslie admitted sheepishly. "That's the good thing about having your child be your designated driver." She poked her elbow playfully into Kerry's ribs.

As her parents and Leslie moved toward the table of food, Gwen leaned over to Kerry. "I spiked the punch. I love getting them in trouble."

"You guys are great. I wish my family was more like yours." For the first time the bright smile faded from Kerry's face.

"We're all family now." She slung an arm over Kerry's slight shoulder. "Forget those cookies, I'll show you where the good snacks are. The kitchen is so small we keep them in the oven."

The rest of the introductions weren't as painful as Gwen had imagined. Her brothers were their playful, sweet selves. They only told a couple of stupid jokes and, in actuality, it helped break the ice. The other guests behaved themselves too, staring for a bit at first, but quickly moving on to some other topic of gossip.

Gwen felt relief as she grabbed a handful of chips someone had ripped open and left on the table, no time for a bowl. The anxiety she'd felt about blending these two groups had begun to fade. A couple reassuring glances from Griff and his cheeky smile helped.

The sense of calm faded, however, as Leslie approached, her face looking tired and grim. She'd had a good amount of punch, but still her posture was stiff and worried.

"Can we talk for a minute?" she asked, her voice small and far off.

"Sure," Gwen said, choking down a mouthful of chips. "What's up?"

"In private." Leslie pursed her lips and rocked nervously from her toes to her heels.

"There's not a lot of privacy in this little house. Should we go for a walk around the block?" Gwen gestured to the back gate.

"Sure." Leslie looked over her shoulder at Kerry, who had settled in nicely with a couple of Gwen's younger cousins. "I don't mean to be dramatic."

"I could use a walk anyway." Gwen shrugged. "I ate way too much."

"You all have me questioning Kerry's graduation dinner. She's going to hate it compared to this." Leslie let out a little laugh.

"The grass is always greener at that age," Gwen said, waving the idea off. "Whatever you plan will be perfect."

They made their way out the back gate and across the neighbor's lot to the street. It was quiet. Peaceful. Gwen felt the pressure between them building and finally she had to ask. "Is everything all right? You seem worn out."

Leslie looked reluctant to speak, but finally licked her dry lips and began. "People aren't supposed to unload their problems on their children."

"I'm a big girl and it's not unloading. I want to know. I care what happens with all of you."

"Things have been rough. Everything with Paul fell apart very quickly. Much faster than I expected. He's not being very mature about this whole thing. My boys are still struggling too. It's not how I pictured Kerry's graduation would be."

"I'm really sorry about that," Gwen said, staring down at the cracks in the asphalt as they walked.

Leslie slapped a hand to her own chest. "Oh, it's not your fault. I hope that's not what you think."

Gwen gave a half smile. She appreciated the attempt, but the truth couldn't be hidden behind kindness. "I can't ignore the fact that I came in and things fell apart from there. It was my biggest fear when I started all of this. I put my own feelings above the damage I might do."

"Your feelings matter. And you did exactly the right thing. I am so happy to know you. To know what a wonderful family you ended up with. It brings me enormous peace. Peace I waited half a lifetime for. What's going on with Paul and me is very different. I'm learning it's all about foundation, and we didn't have a strong one. When that's the case, eventually things crumble. If it weren't for meeting you, it would have been something else. Please don't take any responsibility for that."

"I'm still sorry you're going through this. Is there anything I can do to help?" Gwen tucked her hands into her pockets, not wanting to scratch nervously at her cuticles. It was a habit she needed to break.

Ironically, Leslie began needling at her own thumb. Her words came out tentatively. "I gave you some information on Mark."

The knot in Gwen's stomach pulled even tighter. "You gave me his name."

"You couldn't do anything with it? Your tenacity has amazed me so far. I figured you'd have met him by now." Leslie gave a playful smile, but her eyes stayed sad. "You know, I look at you and see so much of myself. So much of who I might have been if things were different. I look at you and Kerry and feel so hopeful that you won't make the mistakes I did."

Gwen couldn't help but wonder if her birth was in the mistake column when Leslie tallied that up. Pretending to be fascinated by the honeysuckle bushes they passed, Gwen reported back the same thing she told anyone who asked about Mark. "Unfortunately it's too common of a name. The parts of California he lived in back then have too many possibilities for me to narrow down. Plus, he could have moved away. Needle in a haystack. It's all right though. It's just not meant to be. Don't let that add more stress for you. I'm happy to have found you." Gwen was terrified to go through it all again. No matter how many times people told her the aftermath of her choices weren't her fault, she felt the pins and needles of worry pricking her.

Leslie hugged her arms around her waist as if she had a chill. "I want you to find him. I carried this around with me alone for a long time. It wore me down in a lot of ways. I let it. Crossing over this bridge, to the side of truth, has helped. It's just not finished yet. But I could have done more to help you find Mark. The problem is, there are parts of that story I haven't thought about in years. And he'll be one more person I'll have to answer to for my choice. I can't begin to know how he'll react, but I'm sure I'll take the brunt of that reaction."

"I don't want you to go through that. You gave me what you had on him and it didn't work out. Maybe we should let it go."

"I could have gotten more creative. I owe you both that. Mark was an incredible man. To this day, one of the best I've ever met. You deserve to know him, and he deserves to know you. I don't know if I'll find peace without that."

Gwen had a million questions, but no way to ask them. As she struggled to make sense of the rush of thoughts and attempted to form words around them, one thought was louder than the rest, drowning them out like a car alarm blaring in her mind. "He may not want that. Look at how much your life has changed over the years since my adoption. His likely has too. Even if I can't take all the responsibility for your current situation, I have to be honest enough with myself and admit I played a part. I'm not sure I'm ready to do that again." Gwen hadn't admitted that to anyone. "I can't stroll into another family and act like anything but a wrecking ball."

Leslie didn't argue. She nodded as though something had just become abundantly clear. "I get it. Trust me, I under-stand exactly what you're saying. Most days I just want to hide out. It's like the emotional equivalent of an airplane circling the skies above the airport, waiting for the storm to pass. But eventually it'll run out of fuel."

Gwen exhaled, sorrow filling her chest. This was all supposed to be easier. Fulfilling. Not so scary. She'd found what she was looking for, but it was messier than she'd hoped.

Stopping in her tracks and turning toward Gwen, Leslie spoke with confidence finally. "I called the company Mark worked for when we knew each other. I got his middle name."

"How?" Gwen felt her heart skip a beat.

"I lied. Made up some story about old tax papers that needed to be sorted out for my former employer. I probably broke a law or two."

"You didn't have to do that."

"It's what you would have done if you weren't so afraid. Back in December, when you were looking for me, nothing would stop you. I don't want to be the reason you're hesitating. Could it be messy? Maybe. But that's no reason to freeze up. Not now. I like to believe that some of your tenacity comes from me. I don't want my issues to be what takes that from you. I made the call you would have."

"It was twenty-seven years ago; they fell for that?" Gwen eyed Leslie with bewilderment.

She blushed. "I was very convincing. They didn't have any further information they were willing to provide. But his middle name is Armand. His first name is actually Markus. I bet that would narrow your search down quite a bit."

"It would."

"Then land the plane, Gwen. Stop circling. I know it's scary. I wake up every day a little terrified, but I'm still here. Still a mother. Still a friend. My career is going well. I have to mourn my marriage. I have to face my choices and the way they impact my family. But I still have a lot to wake up for, and a lot to fight for. You're one of the things I'm fighting for. I feel like you need a little push here."

"I do." Gwen nodded.

"You just graduated. You're moving back to this beautiful house, working at a new lab. You have the foundation I never created for myself. Maybe things will get a bit shaken up, but what you have will stay standing. I think in your heart you know that."

Gwen opened her mouth to argue but couldn't. Leslie was correct. While the Fox family had been rocked by the tremors of Gwen's decisions, they were still here. Still laughing. And eventually things would settle back down. They'd be all right.

She had Mark's full name, something that would surely make finding him easier. No excuses now.

"Just think on it," Leslie pleaded.

"How can you be so sure he's still such a great man? Over a quarter century later and you're certain?"

"Our time together was brief but impactful. No matter what's happened to him over the years, I have to believe he has the same big heart." Leslie pulled her hands over her chest and drew in a deep breath. "He was something special. Just like you."

As they rounded the corner, approaching the front of Gwen's house, she saw Griff sitting on the steps mindlessly pulling a couple of weeds that had sprouted through the cement.

"Looks like someone else wants to take a stroll with you," Leslie said, finally perking up a bit. "He seems like a great friend."

"He is," Gwen said, relieved Leslie had called him a friend, not taking the easy shot by implying it was more.

"I had a lot of plans for my kids. Visions of what they'd accomplish. I poured a lot of energy, mostly unnecessary energy, into those goals. They didn't get a sports scholarship. The music lessons didn't result in a seat in an orchestra. If I could go back, I would have spent more time on one lesson."

"Just one?" Gwen drew her brows together and eyed Leslie. How could life be boiled down to just one thing?

"Surprisingly, yes. I wish I'd told them not to settle. In relationships. In opportunities. Even in their expectations of themselves. I wish I had held myself to that standard. Things might have been different for all of us if I had."

As they approached the front of the house, Leslie gave a small wave to Griff before pulling Gwen in for a hug. "I'll find my way back to the party. You two should talk." Heading around the side of the house to the gate, Leslie looked a little brighter, her shoulders not so heavily weighed down. As if handing that information to Gwen was in some way unburdening herself.

"Have a nice walk?" Griff asked, patting the hard cement of the steps next to him and inviting her to sit.

"She found Mark's full name," Gwen explained, twisting her mouth to the side as if the words were sour. "It should make finding my biological father easier."

"Good," Griff said, standing since she decided not to sit by him. "When do we leave?"

"Right," she snickered. "You had a hard time getting away for this party. You can't come to California on such short notice."

"Let me worry about that. Can you get away now?"

"I have two weeks before my job starts. I had planned to just take my time moving and unpacking."

"Perfect." He took one of her hands in his. "I've got a lot

of flight points, I'll cover the tickets. It might have to be a red-eye or something though."

She squeezed his hand. "You are not beholden to some agreement we made months ago. Things are different now."

"What's different?" His eyes raked over her face, a hopeful glint sparkling.

"Well, you know . . ." She gestured something erratic with her hands as if that would clear things up.

"You've lost that loving feeling for me?" He feigned distress as he covered his heart with his hands.

"Shut up. Things are different because we have things going on in our lives now. I can't tell you how much it meant to me to have you by my side through everything. I don't know if I would have made it without you."

"Then let's do it again." His voice was cool and easy, which only made her worry more. Didn't he understand this could be complicated? A mess. Maybe worse this time.

"I haven't decided if I'm going to go out there," she admitted sheepishly. "Didn't you see Leslie today? She looks exhausted. Her boys are barely talking to her. It's going to ruin Kerry's graduation."

"And obviously you should shoulder all the blame for that." He kept his expression level.

"I'm not exactly ready to go do it all again. That's all I'm saying. Maybe I need time to process finding Leslie before I look for Mark."

He nodded as though he understood but turned his attention to his phone while she continued.

"It's not a sprint, it's a marathon. I haven't even met my brothers yet. I should just focus on that for now. Maybe settle in at work. Spend some time this summer with Kerry." She ticked the list off on her fingers and narrowed her eyes as Griff let himself be distracted. "Are you even listening to me? I'm making a plan."

"I just booked two tickets to Los Angeles. Make sure you're ready to go in two days." He tucked his phone in his pocket and winked. "You don't know how much time you have for any of this. It would be awful if you put it off and then found out you missed the opportunity to meet him."

"We haven't found him yet," she squeaked, her cheeks glowing pink with anger. "Maybe he's not in California anymore."

"The tickets are transferable, but not refundable. Wherever he is, we're going. You have his middle name now. So start looking for him. I know if anyone can track him down it's you."

She leaned back and eyed him from head to toe. "You are out of your mind. Don't you ever think about consequences, or the odds stacked against you?"

"Odds are only there to be beaten." He marched up the steps and kept a hand on the screen door as he looked back at her. "Nothing has changed, Gwen. Not for me."

CHAPTER THREE

Mark pulled his sports car into the parking lot of the high school. The Performing Arts building was small and his only option was to park sandwiched between two dented mini-vans. The passenger seat held the comically large bouquet of lilies he'd ordered. It was ironic that Jane had normally taken care of such things. Floral arrangements, thank you cards, condolences. Appraising the giant bouquet, he knew he did well. All on his own.

Settling into a chair near the front, he thought of all the theater performances he'd begrudgingly gone to over the years. Broadway. Famous shows. The operas he'd escorted clients to. It was always terribly inconvenient to have to turn his phone off for that length of time. The Asian market could tank. News of the latest acquisition could break. And he'd be sitting in a tuxedo, watching people pretend on a stage. It always felt like a trivial distraction.

Tonight there was no rush. He was glad to turn his phone off. To focus all his attention on the stage as the dancers tip-toed their way out in the darkness and stood as still as statues.

It took a few moments to discern which silhouette belonged to Marisa. It wasn't until the low light came on that he was sure. She had Jane's distinct smile and dainty nose.

Laying the lilies on the seat next to him, he gave a small nod. Marisa stood stoically, her arms over her head, waiting for the music to begin. But her eyes smiled and he knew she was pleased to see him. Jane had been right.

For the first time in his life he watched the stage without his mind wandering to some other responsibility. He watched every nuanced bit of the performance. He listened to the music rise and fall in a way he'd never bothered to before. It was a simple performance, based loosely on a fairy tale he'd forgotten the name of. Perched on an unforgiving folding chair in a stuffy high school building, Mark took time to notice the battle of good and evil and the triumphant victory of everlasting love. The set was cobbled together pieces of painted wood, yet his new, relaxed perspective meant he could see royal celebrations in a magnificent castle.

Marisa played a beautiful part and it pained Mark to realize he was the only one in the audience for her. Jane should be here. That stupid ex-husband of hers should have come too. Mark understood life could be unfair. When he was Marisa's age his family never could have afforded to even participate in any extracurricular activities. He just wished things were different for Jane.

When the curtain dropped and the performance ended, Mark found himself clapping enthusiastically, nearly rising to his feet before he realized no one else was. Instead, he grabbed the flowers and waited patiently. A few other people in the crowd complimented the floral arrangement as they looked down at their own far more modest ones.

It wasn't until fifteen minutes had passed and most of the room had cleared out that he started to wonder if he should go too. Maybe Marisa was still in back even though it seemed as though all the other dancers had come to greet their friends and family.

"Excuse me, are you Mr. Ruiz?" A tiny framed girl with red frizzy hair tapped his shoulder and whispered quietly to him.

"Yes," he replied tentatively as he rose to his feet.

"I'm Darla. Marisa's friend. She came here with my family today."

"Oh, nice to meet you, Darla. You all put on a very nice show."

Darla fidgeted, looking unsure how to proceed. "Marisa is still in the dressing room. She's pretty upset but she didn't want you waiting for her. She felt bad."

"What is she upset about?" Mark asked, looking around the room of other dancers who were chatting loudly. They didn't seem distressed at all.

Darla lowered her voice. "I told her I wouldn't say anything, but I'm not sure what to do. Maybe I should let my mom know."

"What happened?"

Darla handed over a crumpled piece of paper and continued to stare at the ground.

Flattening it in his hands, he read the note.

Why are you even here? You are too fat to dance. No one wants you on the stage. Not even your own family. They don't even bother coming.

Mark's stomach dropped as he crumpled the paper tightly in his fist. "Who wrote this?"

"I don't know," Darla squeaked like a cornered mouse. "A lot of the girls have been mean to Marisa lately. She's been trying to ignore it all, but they won't stop."

"Who?" Mark scanned the room as though he'd be able to spot the mean girls. "Go tell Marisa I'd like to see her. I know she's upset but tell her it's important."

"It's mostly them over there. Those five or six girls." Darla nodded and hurried off as Mark moved closer to a few of the chatting groups around him, hoping to hear something incriminating.

When Marisa emerged, her eyes were ringed red and her shoulders slumped. "Hi, Mark."

"Hey kiddo. Great performance."

"These flowers are beautiful," she choked out, but he didn't hand them over. "You didn't have to come. I know you are busy. Did my mom make you?"

"Make me? Marisa, I really enjoyed the performance."

She rolled her eyes as though she knew it was a lie.

"Can I be honest with you?" Mark asked, lowering his voice. "Retirement has been awful. I'm going crazy just looking out over that stupid lake. Most days I sit around alone wondering what the hell I was thinking leaving work. It's painful."

"Really?" she asked, twisting her little face up at him curiously. "You hate it?"

"I hate it. Don't tell your mom."

"Sorry. That sucks."

"This note sucks," he said, holding up the crumpled paper.

"Darla showed you? I told her not to."

"I'm glad she did," Mark said, raising his voice. "It gives

me the opportunity to do this. Excuse me." He waved his hands and moved to the front of the room. "Can I have everyone's attention please?"

Heads began to turn his way and a hush fell over the dancers and their remaining guests who had stayed in the room.

"My name is Mark Ruiz, I'm a representative for the National Dance Academy Club, New York Chapter." Now he had their attention. Their angelic little faces were trained on him. Their hopeful looking parents had even quieted enough to tune in. "I really enjoyed the show this evening." Their smiles grew. "Though as I'm sure anyone in the audience could tell there is room for improvement. A few stumbles." He gestured subtly with his chin at one girl who Darla had outed as the bully. "And some who need to work on their form." He moved his eyes to a few other girls. "But there were also some very bright lights of talent on that stage. As many of you already know, the NDCA often makes a habit of bringing flowers and presenting them to the performer who represents our standards of excellence." He was almost surprised how easy it was. How quickly they all inched in closer and held their delicate chins in the air.

Mark had spent a lifetime making deals happen and creating cohesive teams. And the one truth that carried over to every situation was this: people wanted to be noticed. To feel special. A singular prize from a place with a fancy acronym for a name could do just that.

"Miss," he said, turning toward Marisa and handing over the flowers. "This dance troupe is lucky to have you on stage. I hope they realize that. I'd love to get the contact information for your parents. We'll be in touch." He bowed a bit and turned back to the other dancers and their parents. "The rest of you girls keep working hard. Encourage each other. We are always on the lookout for improved talent, but most importantly for young people with heart. A team is built on more than just what happens on that stage. It's how you all treat each other. Trust me. I've been doing this job a long time. I can spot a unified team from a mile away."

Without another word, he turned and headed out of the auditorium and into the brightness of the parking lot. Mark's grin was so wide he almost didn't recognize himself as he caught his reflection in the shine of his car's paint. These were the skills he missed using. Confidence. Charisma. Some little white lies that were for the greater good.

He was twenty minutes down the road back toward his house when his phone rang.

"You're something else," Jane said with a sigh. "That could have really backfired if anyone besides Darla knew who you were."

"Did they?" Mark asked through a wry smile. "I thought they all fell for it."

"Hook, line, and sinker. They're all clamoring to get a look at those flowers you brought and complimenting the hell out of my daughter all of a sudden."

"That note was abhorrent." He ground his teeth as he thought of it again.

"High school girls are ruthless. Today they don't like Marisa, and they'll find some other target tomorrow. It's like the wild west out there, Mark."

"I'm sorry if I overstepped. I just couldn't bear to see her hurting like that. Not at the hands of those smug little jerks."

"You didn't overstep. Marisa was throwing around the word hero. They'll leave her alone for a little while."

"Only a little while?"

"Unfortunately, that's how it works. But for today you fixed it. We don't get a lot of chances to do that. I really appreciate you being there and helping her when she needed it. You've always been there for us."

"I'm realizing now, more than ever, it was you who was there for me. I look back on my career, and a good portion of my success can be contributed to your skills. I wish I'd told you that more often."

"Are you all right?" Jane's voice fell quiet. "Is this a twelve-step program or something? Making amends? You sound different."

"I feel different," he admitted, and allowed her to assume different meant better.

Jane laughed. "I just got a text from Marisa. Two girls just invited her to a party next week. Your plan seems to have worked."

"Good. You've raised great girls. They deserve the best. They're lucky to have you. I was way out of my depth in there today."

"You'd have been a great father if that was what you wanted. Any kid would have been lucky to have you."

"Oh, you know me, I'm a rolling stone. No time to settle down."

"You'll have time now," Jane retorted.

"I'm a little old for kids don't you think?"

"Maybe," Jane replied coolly. She drew in a deep breath as though readying herself to say something she'd always wanted to. "But you're not too old to find someone to settle down with. I never understood why you were single all this time. You know I wouldn't judge you if you preferred the company of men. I know in your industry there can be some old school opinions on the matter. I don't hold those opinions."

"That's sweet of you, Jane. You've sent enough flowers for me over the years to know I fancy women. But I've never had quite enough to give to make it work with anyone long term. Or maybe I've just never been willing to give it."

"You should try. It doesn't have to be a romantic relation-ship. Just let your guard down with someone. Anyone. You have so much to offer. I've always considered you a friend, but you have some major walls up. I want you to be happy."

"You've been dying to tell me all that, haven't you?" He chuckled, letting her off the hook with some levity.

"Only the last ten years or so. But it's much easier now that you don't sign my paycheck."

"Well I'll take your advice into consideration. Maybe it's time to take a few bricks out of the wall."

CHAPTER FOUR

"I'm sorry, I'm just having a hard time keeping up with your choices," Millie said, using the scissors to cut open another box. They'd begun unpacking Gwen's belongings as all of her parents' things had been moved to the condo. "It's dizzying how often you change your mind. I think I liked it better when you had a rigid plan for your life. You were boring, but I always knew what to expect."

"Boring?" Gwen pretended to be insulted but she knew what her mother meant. And to be honest, in a way, she missed those days too.

"I meant it as a compliment," Millie teased. "Reliably boring."

Gwen hardly recognized the house without any of her parents' trinkets and decorations. The bare walls didn't seem like a blank canvas awaiting her personal touch. Instead they were just reminders of how her things would look like odd replacements. She didn't have antique pieces with character or matching sets of anything. It felt like she was five again, trying to march around in her mother's high-heeled boots, playing at adulthood.

"I have new information. That's why I changed my mind about California. Leslie gave me a middle name. I think I found Mark. That's why I'm going."

"With Griff." Millie kicked her chin out and raised a brow. "The person with whom nothing is going on."

"With whom? Really. Mom, it's not a big deal. No need to launch a formal investigation. I can't tell you what's going on between Griff and me because I have no clue. We had decided it wasn't the right time to try to put a label on anything. Not until things settle down."

"I spent half my life telling people, 'I'm very busy this week but by next week things should settle down.' That has yet to happen. You can't live your life waiting for the eye of the storm."

Gwen let out a loud groan. "Please don't let the next words out of your mouth be that I should go dance in the rain rather than waiting for the storm to pass." Teasing Millie about her cliché advice was a favorite family pastime. Favorite for everyone but Millie.

"Of course not. That's dumb. You'll catch a cold if you dance in the rain."

"Actually you catch a cold from germs. It's a myth that being out in bad weather makes you sick."

"This house is too small for your master's degree. Leave it at the door, will you?"

She loved to be playfully sparring with her mother again. This journey, the one she'd started, had sprinkled eggshells between them. For a little while it made every step tentative. Now things were getting back to normal. Just in time for

Gwen to disrupt them again with another trip toward her past.

"I'm sorry if you don't want me to go to California." Gwen softened her expression. Millie certainly earned a break by now. But that break wasn't coming.

"I just thought we'd spend the next couple of weeks unpacking and getting the house ready. Now it's just going to be me and your father in that little condo." Millie flopped onto the couch and looked around the room as if the ghosts of their past were swirling around them. This was where she'd raised her family. Spent what she called the best years of her life. Leaving must be daunting.

"The condo is very nice, Mom. You and Dad have plenty of friends who could come over and keep you company. It'll be fine."

"And now you'll be gone for Kerry's graduation dinner, and I'll have to go without you. Your father is terrible at those things. He always tells the joke about the hamster even when I beg him not to. And I'm sure the food will be fancy. We'll have to stop for burgers on the way so we don't starve to death. Maybe it's not the right time to go to California."

"And I might find Mark." Gwen sat down next to her mother and moaned. "You could talk me out of going. I've been changing my mind every few hours. You're right. It is dizzying."

Millie leaned her head on Gwen's shoulder. "Don't tell me that. You know I won't actually talk you out of going. I'm just complaining. You have to go. If you don't, you'll always wonder what you might have found there. And Mark deserves to know what an amazing child he helped create."

"I'm sorry the timing isn't better. I just need to deal with this before I start work. I want a clean slate for the next part of my life."

"Are you in love with Griff?" Millie lifted her head but didn't fix her eyes on her daughter. Likely afraid a hard stare would scare her from answering.

"Mom!" Gwen jolted, stalling for time. It was a question she wouldn't even ask herself. There was no good answer. Did love matter if you weren't going to do anything about it? "I've told you a thousand times what's going on with Griff and me. At the moment, nothing."

"Gwen." Millie turned and pulled her daughter's chin toward her gaze. "You need to figure that out. You need to get to the real answer. I'm going to keep asking the question until you do. I know when you're young you feel invincible. Like opportunities are boundless. The next one will be right around the corner. But you'll have to take my word for it, at some point the corners get few and far between. And sometimes what's right in front of you is perfect. I don't want you to have regrets."

"What do you regret?" Gwen tried to turn the tables. But Millie was too skilled for that maneuver.

"Nothing I took a risk on. I'm not telling you what to do, I'm just warning you against doing nothing. Sometimes it feels easier to sit back and decide what is meant to be will be."

"It's in a song. It must be true. You disagree?"

"Completely. What's meant to be should be chased. Full speed and tackled to the ground. Passively waiting never got anyone anything."

Noel was smart enough to whistle a causal little tune before barging into the living room and interrupting. It was a familiar tactic of his. It gave them time to change the subject if it was some kind of lady business they were discussing. The song was just enough to announce his arrival. "What are my two best ladies talking about?"

"Regrets," Millie said, playfully nudging Gwen.

"Oh boy. I had better not be on that list." He furrowed his bushy brows together. "I had better be on the 'best thing that ever happened to you' list."

"You know it." Millie blew a kiss. "We were talking more about Gwen going to California tomorrow."

"That's back on?" Noel's mouth turned downward. "That's good."

"You don't look like it's good news." Gwen felt her chest grow tight. She wanted to assure him that in her heart he was her father. The only man she'd ever see that way. No matter what she found in California, that wouldn't change.

Noel had the credentials. His *dad résumé* was loaded with experience and expertise. He chased away monsters with monster spray. Bedtime stories were epic tales that always somehow included her as the main character. No matter how long his workday lasted he found the energy to regale her with a wild story that ended up filling her dreams with happy thoughts. No one tucked her in tighter, going around the bed twice to make sure she was snug. No one made her feel safer.

His remedy for her bad mood was bad jokes. Shockingly, it usually worked. She'd laugh in spite of herself. A jack of all trades, there was nothing Noel couldn't fix. A broken fence post or a broken heart always mended when he took on the job. His pep talks were legendary. Over-the-top proclamations that bolstered her confidence. When Noel told her she was good enough, she believed him. When he reminded her of what she deserved, she felt compelled to demand it of the world.

Even the areas where he was less than an expert made him more endearing. His sense of fashion was ghastly but his sense of humor was timeless. He blushed and blustered when any discussion of menstruation came up. But he'd also slide a chocolate bar under her bedroom door when he knew she had cramps. One time when Millie was visiting a friend overnight in Rhode Island and Gwen ran out of tampons he took on the job, though he'd looked like a soldier readying for war. He brought back one of everything, including a pack of adult diapers, just to be safe. Noel wasn't perfect, but he gave the perfect amount of effort all the time.

There would be nothing on the other side of the country, or anywhere in the world for that matter, that would compete with her father. He was the man for the job. Qualified. Fortified. Irreplaceable.

So why don't I try to tell him all of that?

Simple. He'd never give her a chance to get past the first sentence. He didn't need the boost to his heart. It was strong enough to bear the pain of competition, and that's what made him so special. No matter how much his body had begun giving out on him, he was still the strongest man Gwen would ever know. The heaviest burdens of their lives were always shouldered by Noel. Maybe some parents wouldn't lay their life down for their children, but Noel was ready to give every ounce of himself. It was more than just being a shield against danger. It was unending stamina for being their father. Tireless when he was exhausted. Dogged when they needed him to be. And most of all when he should have had nothing left to go around, he always found more of himself to give.

"I'll give you a ride to the airport tomorrow," he said, plastering on a smile. "What time is your flight?"

"You'd have to ask Griff," Millie teased. "He booked the flights for them. The two of them are running off together."

"Oh, this again." Noel gave a hearty laugh. "I'll definitely take you two to the airport tomorrow. It'll give me a chance to have the, 'What are your intentions with my daughter?' conversation again. Apparently he's not gotten the hint yet."

"Your hints are not very subtle, Dad." Gwen stood and kissed his cheek. The assurance of her love, all the words she wanted to say, were conveyed perfectly in that tiny kiss. He squeezed her tightly and winced a bit at his back pain.

"Maybe your other dad has a stronger back. He had a twenty-six-year vacation from you. After you find him, have him swing by and put that bookshelf together in your bedroom."

"I'm not getting my hopes up. He might want to extend his vacation from me another twenty-six years," Gwen admitted quietly, still hugging her dad tightly.

"Then he's a fool, and I'll make sure Griff pops him one for me. Right in that big nose." Noel stepped back and put his fist up.

"How do you know he has a big nose?" Gwen leaned away and eyed him, knowing damn well his jokes were coming. There was always a mischievous expression that preceded a dad joke.

"That must be where you got your big schnoz from," he replied, straight-faced. What made the joke funny was the fact that Gwen's nose wasn't big at all. The Fox family never took aim at people's true weaknesses.

Gwen covered her face with her hand. "My nose is not big." She looked to her mother, demanding an ally.

Millie faked some righteous indignation for her daughter's sake. "Noel. Don't say that. They call that a distinguished nose. Not big."

"You two know I can kick you out of this house now, right? It's mine. All the paperwork has been signed. You're technically trespassing." Gwen propped a hand up on her hip and pointed toward the door. "There are no big noses at your condo. Feel free to go there."

Noel shrugged as he reached a hand down to his wife. "Well, Mr. Carlyle has a pretty substantial one. Not as big as yours, but close. The good news is he and his wife have been married for fifty-three years so there is still hope for you."

"You have to behave if you plan to take us to the airport tomorrow," Gwen threatened as she walked them both to the door. This would be her first night in the house without them. This would be their first night in their new condo. It was clear they were all questioning whether they'd made the right choices.

"I promise to be good."

"His fingers are crossed behind his back," Millie reported in a whisper.

"I know. He can't behave. But I wouldn't expect anything different." Gwen took one last hug from each of them.

"You can text Griff now. Tell him he can come over." Millie gave a sly grin.

Gwen waved her hand dismissively as they headed out. "He's not coming over tonight."

Millie laughed. "Sure he's not. But if he was coming over, he'd probably be hungry. I made you two a potpie. It's in the fridge. Read the directions I left on top. Don't burn it by putting the oven up too hot."

Noel spoke over his shoulder as he reached his car door. "Don't let anything get too hot tonight. I could be back at any moment to pick up something I forgot."

"I'm changing the locks," Gwen called out through a smile. "Maybe getting an alarm system."

"You know your mother will ninja her way right through that thing to bring you a meatloaf. She's a very determined woman. That's where you get it from."

"And yet we're still no match for you." Gwen waved goodbye, sadness creeping in and making her eyes water.

"Don't forget that." He winked and waved as he settled gingerly into the driver's seat of the car.

She wondered how much longer he'd be able to comfortably drive. What would it be like when her mother had to take over? What other powerful traits of his would this intolerable pain greedily sponge up?

Gwen wanted her father to forever be the man he had always been. The one who saved her from that mean dog in the neighborhood that snapped at her arm. The one who grabbed her coat when she nearly walked off the train platform in the city. Those were the building blocks he was made of. His reflexes. His strong arms. A tool belt loaded down with a well-worn hammer and a handful of nails. A skilled driver who could navigate even the most aggressive traffic. Nothing rattled him. There wasn't a sport he couldn't play well or a household job he couldn't tackle.

Now he was moving to a condo because it had a

handyman and a landscaping company. It made her sad. Then she realized the other thing that made him who he was. With all he was losing, he wasn't sad. Or he wasn't putting that burden of his sadness on them. Noel, even in his weakened state, was finding ways to be impossibly strong.

Gwen reached for her phone and sent the text.

Gwen: My parents just left. My mom made us a potpie.
  Griff: Be there soon. Don't burn it.

CHAPTER FIVE

Mark

The voice-mail icon on his phone was flashing. Mark let his finger hover over the delete button.

Hi, Mark. I'm not sure if you got my letters. I'm not trying to pester you. I was just hoping you'd have called by now. I found your business phone number online. I called and they gave me your personal cell number. If you could just—

Delete.

This girl was relentless. He pushed the thought out of his mind as he slung his golf clubs into the back of his car. It had been a blazing hot day on the course, and he was exhausted. The people he'd been paired with, a husband and wife on their anniversary trip, were equally as draining as the relentless sun. They looked at him like he was from another planet when he told them he had never married and had no children. Parting with them on the eighteenth hole had felt liberating.

Bye, Stan and Martha. Don't call me.

"Excuse me," a woman's voice carried across the parking lot. She was waving her hand frantically at him. "Do you have jumper cables by any chance?" Her tennis clothes were rimmed with sweat and the expression on her face was harried. He guessed she was younger than him by a handful of years.

"Uh, I do." He shoved his clubs to the side and saw the cables coiled up in the trunk. "You have a dead battery?"

The woman's eyes were wet with the shadow of tears. She pulled her visor off her head and let her thick blonde hair free. "I think so. I tried to call a tow truck but they said it would be over an hour. I have a dinner to get to." She checked her watch and then looked up at him helplessly.

"I can give you a jump. It's no problem."

She gestured over to her shiny red convertible. "Are you sure?"

He nodded and grabbed the jumper cables. Even though he was overheated and dying for a cold beer, he couldn't say no. Mark had a reputation. His friends said he was a magnet for women in need. Damsels in distress. But that wasn't the case. They weren't drawn to him, he just said yes when they needed help. Because people had always helped his mother, and he knew that was what got him to where he was today.

Kindness to a woman who was doing her best, but still coming up short.

"I didn't know people knew how to do this anymore," she said through a laugh as he pulled his car over to hers. "I sure don't know how to use jumper cables."

"I'm not sure if young people do anymore. But I haven't been accused of being a young person for a while." He watched with pleasant bemusement as she snickered coyly at his joke. Her little laugh was refreshingly bright, considering her situation.

"My name is Jocelyn." Seeming suddenly self-conscious, she shifted her tennis shirt and tried to pat down her wild hair. There was no need. She was gorgeous, and the glistening sweat on her skin only added to her beauty.

"I'm Mark." He popped her hood and got to work. Truthfully it had been a while since he'd had to do anything mechanical. He had a guy for that. He had someone for almost all his needs these days. But the days of trying to keep his mother's latest busted-up, tin can car moving came right back to him. If it wasn't the battery, he'd just whack the starter with a rock, like the good old days. "You'll want to keep it running awhile after we start it. Give the battery a chance to charge back up."

"You're a lifesaver." Jocelyn covered her heart with her hands gratefully. He kept his eyes on the task at hand but as her perfume wafted over to him he decided to turn on the charm. He'd been holed up lately doing a lot of nothing. Flirting wasn't a skill he wanted to get rusty.

"I don't want you to miss that important dinner. Your date would be disappointed." He never had a pole, but he was always great at fishing for information.

Jocelyn blushed, her pale ivory skin blazing for a moment then settling back. "It's not a date. It's a job interview."

"Well you can't miss that either. What do you do for work?" Mark attached the cables to both cars and finally took a moment to appraise her. Jocelyn had interesting features. Challenging to pin down her ethnicity. Thin lips and sparkling blue eyes. Toned arms and luscious curves. He hadn't seen her at the clubhouse before. Jocelyn was the kind of woman he'd remember. Not for her beauty, though she had that in spades. The part of her he would be able to spot as memorable was her guarded expression. There was something kindred between them he couldn't quite name. A pain boxed up and tucked away.

"I haven't done anything for work in a very long time," she admitted sheepishly. "In another life I worked retail. That was before I married a high-powered lawyer and gave it all up."

He glanced at her hand and didn't see a ring. He thought he saw her glance at his too. This was turning into quite the dance. "You have the sudden urge to get back to work?"

"Necessity. My husband decided his twenty-six-year-old secretary had a bit more to offer than I did. I signed a prenup before we married. I wasn't worried because obviously we were going to make it for the long haul." She groaned and rolled her eyes. "I was the same age as his secretary is now when I signed that stupid thing. Like I said, he's a very good lawyer. I won't end up with much of anything. So I need to get to dinner and land this job."

"I'm sorry to hear that. What a jackass." Mark rubbed at the sweat on his forehead.

"Oh, you smudged grease on you." Jocelyn reached into

her car and grabbed a small towel from her tennis bag. Without any hesitation she stretched up and wiped the smudge away, her hand lingering for a moment.

"Thanks. I hope you make it to your interview and it works out for you."

"I'm trying to stay positive. This company I'm interviewing for seems promising."

"You're getting back into retail?"

"No. It's actually a connection I made here at the club. A marketing firm that needs some fresh perspectives. Nicolas says I have something they've been looking for."

This time it was Mark who checked his watch. He'd interviewed hundreds of people during his career. Taking a beautiful, but underqualified woman to dinner at six-thirty at night didn't exactly meet the standards of a formal interview. It was usually sinister.

He wracked his brain for club members who might be the culprit. "Nicolas Epstein?"

"Yes. You know him?" Jocelyn lit with excitement as though this acknowledgment lent credibility to her plans.

He almost uttered the word: unfortunately. Instead he just nodded and leaned into her car to try the ignition. She stood close to him, crossing her fingers like a hopeful child. When the car roared to life, she squealed excitedly.

"There you go," he said with a cool shrug. "All set."

"Thank you." She squeezed his arm and her lashes fluttered as she batted away the hint of nervous tears. "Can I ask you a question?"

"As long as it's not about cars." He chuckled. "That's about the extent of my mechanic skills."

Jocelyn's expression was suddenly filled with concern.

"Do you think it's odd that Nicolas asked me to dinner to talk about work? He's a married man so I don't think it's anything scandalous. I'm not a twenty-six-year-old secretary so I wouldn't be any fun to pursue."

"Not all men think younger women are superior." He gave a serious look that let her know he certainly didn't. "Some of us know that experience is paramount."

She hummed her approval. "I was having a drink in the clubhouse after tennis last week. I think people know about my husband by now. Maybe Nicolas is just being nice."

"Epstein? No, I doubt he's just being nice. I've played a few rounds with him. I don't want to color your impression before dinner, but I'll just say, he's not that admirable." Mark wanted to stay out of it. Mind his business. But he knew Nicolas well enough to understand his intentions. The world was full of men like Nicolas. Locker room talk. Always bragging about their latest conquest. It was juvenile but ever present. There was no job for Jocelyn. Only a quid pro quo. Still it wasn't his problem or his place to intrude.

"Maybe you're the sign of my luck turning around. Look how well this worked out." She gestured at her car. "I was starting to think I'd never catch a break."

Mark reached into his pocket and pulled out his business card. He had a few with the number to his personal cell scratched on the back. "Give me a call if you need anything else. I'm retired now, so it's just my personal number on the back."

"Anything else?" she cocked her head to the side quizzically. "You have other services?"

"Plenty," he winked and she rolled her eyes. "But I

should have said to call me if you want to have dinner sometime. I'd love to take you out."

"A direct man. I like that. I don't see any dating in my future though. I've sworn off of men. No relationships. No offense."

"None taken. I'm not very good with relationships either. But I do like to have dinner with interesting people."

"What's interesting about me?" She blushed again, and he saw her hold her breath while he answered.

"I don't know yet," he admitted. "I think by the time we got through dinner I'd have a good list."

She ran her finger across his business card. "Thank you again, Mark."

"Good luck at your interview." Mark tipped his head and stepped back. "And if you find Nicolas doesn't have honorable intentions, tell him you and I are good friends. That you'd hate to have to tell me what happened."

"Wow." Jocelyn's eyes went wide. "You think that would stop him in his tracks? You must have quite the reputation." She nibbled on her bottom lip.

"No ma'am. Reputations are just opinions generally held about someone. I have a proven track record." With that, he closed her hood and dusted his hands off. "Drive safe."

Jocelyn's smile was still dancing at the edges of his mind, even an hour and a half after they parted ways. He cycled through thoughts of her cheery disposition and stewed in frustration over her situation. Mark had no tolerance for men in powerful positions who exploited people. That applied to her husband as well as Nicolas. Mark had risen to power to help people, not use them for his own desires and then throw them away.

It would be much easier for him to move through relationships, over-promise, and leave a wake of broken hearts behind him. It was his restraint that kept him from that. He took no pleasure in hurting people.

He'd built a fire in the living room hearth and listened to the crackling of the wood as if it were a message. Morse code, trying to advise him in some mysterious way. His glass of red wine paired perfectly with the steak he'd made for dinner. All very elegant, except for the folding TV tray. There was no need to sit at the dining room table. It only made him feel pitiful.

When his phone rang he didn't recognize the number. With the letters and voice mails he'd been getting lately he almost didn't pick up. But the wine had him feeling curious. If he didn't like what the person had to say, he'd just hang up and block the number for next time. Technology was great like that.

"Hello?"

"Mark?" The voice was kind but unfamiliar. His heart thudded with panic and he nearly disconnected the call.

"It's Jocelyn. From the golf course earlier today."

"Oh," he said, sitting up straight and bumping his TV tray table, nearly knocking it over. "How are you?"

"Feeling foolish." Her voice was breathy and annoyed.

Mark stood and paced the room. He always did his best talking while moving around. It got the brain going. "Your interview didn't go as planned?"

"Are you someone who usually says, *I told you so?*"

"Not really." He chuckled. "I find people don't appreciate that much."

"Good. But you were right. Nicolas wasn't intrigued by

my fresh take on marketing. If there is a job, I'm not willing to meet his terms in order to take it."

"That's slimy. I'm sorry that happened." Mark moved to the kitchen and busied himself, wiping the already clean counter down.

"Thank you."

A long pause stretched between them. Was this just a quick call to update him? Mark waited, letting her drive the conversation. Assumptions were dangerous. He could easily commandeer the conversation, but he wanted to know what was on her mind.

"My car's good. The battery is fine now." She stretched the words out as though she were searching for more to say.

"That's great. I was glad to help." Mark circled back to the living room and sipped on his red wine. He could almost picture Jocelyn nervously squirming as she kept him on the line.

"I'd like to take you to dinner, to say thank you." Her voice was smaller now, unsure.

He met it with a resounding, too enthusiastic response. "Yes. That would be great. But it'll be my treat if we go out. I'm old-fashioned like that."

"Well, okay then." She paused again. "I only really had an appetizer before I figured out what Nicolas wanted."

She wanted dinner now?

He looked down at his half-eaten steak and then around the empty room. There was no reason to say no. "You shouldn't go to bed hungry. Have you been to Rosco's?"

"Uh, no, I don't think so? Is it Italian?" He could hear her talking through a smile.

"It's very casual. Don't get me wrong, I love a white tablecloth and too many waiters to count, but Rosco's is an institution. I found it after moving here. It's something you have to experience for yourself."

"That sounds perfect. I can meet you there."

"How about eight?"

"Sure." She hesitated, croaking something out and then stopping.

"What is it?" Her hesitation unnerved him.

"I don't want to give you the wrong impression about going out. Meeting at eight o'clock for dinner. It might imply—"

"No implications at all. I'm not Nicolas. I don't invite people out with some agenda in mind. Just dinner."

"Just dinner," she agreed, her voice sounding cheerier. "I'll see you at eight."

CHAPTER SIX

Mark

"It's a drive-in?" Jocelyn asked through her car window as she pulled in next to him. "I can't believe I didn't know this was here."

Mark liked surprising people. Not always with grand gestures. It was just about that little spark of wonder and knowing he'd created it.

He checked his watch. It was nice to have a reason to put it on again. "The movie should start in about twenty minutes. They only play old black-and-whites. We still have time to hit the concession stand." He gestured up to the little shack in the center of the expansive parking lot. Smoke from the grill billowed up from the back of the building and a line spilled out the door.

"A drive-in?" she questioned again, taking it all in. "You

know these places have kind of a reputation. Some lovers' lane type stuff."

"You can sit in your own car if you like. We can just open our windows and shout at each other if we have anything to say. I'm really just here for the cheese fries." He stepped out and pulled open her car door as he extended his hand to her. There was a flash of hesitation on her face, and he understood it perfectly. Jocelyn had every reason to be leery of men. She'd been burned, and he looked just like the flames that kept doing it to her.

She hummed out her weariness. "Do they put that orange processed cheese and bacon on them?"

"Of course they do." Finally she took his hand and stepped out of the car. Jocelyn was effortlessly beautiful. Her black slacks and flowing blouse were far too formal for their current location but suited her beautifully. Chunky gold earrings and a matching necklace gave her a look of elegance Mark couldn't resist. She was stunning.

"Lead the way." She gestured toward the little building and looped her arm in his when he offered it up. "You take a lot of women here?"

"No. You just struck me as someone who could appreciate it."

"I do?" Her face crumpled with confusion. "I look like I belong at the drive-in? With the three-dollar French fries and free soda refills?"

He laughed but stopped abruptly when she didn't look amused. "No, I didn't say you looked like you belonged anywhere. I said you looked like you could appreciate this place. It's been around for sixty years, almost completely unchanged. Where else do you get to sit in the comfort of your car and watch an old movie while eating a week's worth of calories?"

She didn't reply as she nibbled nervously on her bottom lip.

He squeezed her arm gently with his. "I'm sorry if I read the situation wrong. It's not too late. Le Sen Bistro is only a couple miles from here. They have excellent calamari. No cheese fries." He paused and smirked. "Well they do have some potatoes au gratin, which I guess is close. But we wouldn't order that."

"Are you done?" she asked, throwing him a playful look.

He nodded.

"I would like to eat here. I think it's pretty cool. I just wasn't sure what you thought of me. Sometimes I wonder if people can tell."

"Tell what?"

"That if it weren't for my marriage I'd probably be sustaining myself on cheese fries." She tucked her hair behind her ears. "I come from a modest background. One day my soon-to-be ex-husband, Dillard, came into the bookstore where I worked and I knew who he was. Everyone knew who he was. Rich boy. Drove too fast. Skirted all the rules. I didn't pay any attention to him. Shiny things never drew my consideration." She looked down at her thick, braided gold bracelet and snickered. "They still don't, but I wasn't one to turn away a nice gift."

"I hope I didn't give that impression by picking this place. I really just enjoy it. I thought you might too. You said you didn't want it to be a date, and I would never bring a date here." He nudged her playfully with his arm. They stepped into the small concession shack and the smell of fried food overtook his senses.

"It's all right. It's my own insecurities creeping in. I never felt like I belonged in the circles that Dillard and I ran around in. It's like they could smell the poor on me, no matter how much Dior perfume I wore. I haven't told anyone this, but the divorce, as hard as it is, actually feels kind of freeing. I'm not looking forward to starting over, having to fend for myself again, but there are things I'll be glad to put behind me."

"Like what?" He cut off her answer by ordering some food and then turned back toward her. The start of the movie was always the best part. Old throwback commercials and advertisements to reminisce about.

"I won't miss chitchat at cocktail parties with a bunch of other kept women who have nothing of substance to talk about. Or having to hide my real opinion on something because it would reflect unfavorably on my husband."

"That sounds oppressive." He eyed her skeptically. Nothing about Jocelyn seemed obedient or submissive.

She scoffed. "Don't get me wrong. I'm no wilting flower. I'm a very assertive woman. I didn't take any garbage in my marriage. I just played the part when it came to social standards. People have expectations, and I knew it was a game. I'm very competitive that way."

"You never had children?" He hated that question and hated himself for even asking it. "Sorry, forget that. I never appreciate when people grill me on my situation. I try to make it a point not to do the same."

"No, it's all right. The question doesn't bother me. Dillard was one of seven children. The way he talks about his childhood you would think he was raised in the wild, but with money. He never wanted children. I didn't either. I'd caution you against fishing around for a deeper reason. You'll be disappointed. It just wasn't what I wanted."

"I get the question all the time followed by strange looks and inappropriate judgments. I guess women get it even more."

"We do. There was a time in my life, my thirties and forties, when those comments really bothered me. Now I just smile and nod. I know I made the right choice for myself, and that's what matters."

Jocelyn was refreshing. He couldn't help but think about Jane's suggestion. Taking a few bricks out of the big wall he kept up. He grabbed a red cafeteria-style tray and gathered up their food. He was quick to pay before she could object.

As they stepped back into the refreshing night air, the large screen came to life, but they didn't pick up their pace. Suddenly the advertisements he wanted to see were unimportant. They strolled between the other parked cars and she reached for a French fry off the tray.

"I guess I'll get in your car." She shrugged as though she were giving in. He could tell that it was an act.

"I am holding the food. So I guess maybe I am as bad as Nicolas Epstein. Basically a quid pro quo French fry."

"French fries are a much better deal than he was offering. Nicolas wasn't much of a conversationalist either. You're light-years better in that department too."

"I miss talking to people," he admitted coolly, a twinge of regret once the words were out. He was cracking open a door to something he was trying to keep tucked away.

"You do?" Jocelyn looked concerned. "Retirement not what you expected?"

"It's awful." He opened the passenger door for her and then rounded the car to get in. By the time he sank into the driver's seat and settled the tray of food between them, he considered letting the topic drop.

"Awful?" She looked at him expectantly. "Don't most people look forward to retirement? Relaxation. Freedom."

"Boredom." He munched on the fries and considered how she might view him if he continued. Weak? Complaining about his first-world problems like an entitled jerk. "It could be worse. I'm lucky to even be able to retire."

"Don't do that," she scolded gently. "Don't just shrug it off. If you think retirement is awful, own that. Change something. Go back to work. Don't just pretend it's all fine. Life is too short for that."

"I could go back to work." He took a sip of his soda and thought on it. "I've considered consulting, but I'm not sure I'm relevant enough anymore for that. Technology is moving at lightning speed. If I wanted to keep up I'd have to go back to school. Attend dozens of conferences. I don't want that pace back."

"Maybe you just need a hobby." She crossed her beautiful legs and moved her seat back so she could see the screen better.

"There used to be plenty of things I thought I would do after I retired. The list of stuff I convinced myself I'd have time for *someday*. Books I would read just for pleasure. Skills I would improve. I haven't touched the list. It's only been about three months, but I can't seem to figure out my next move."

"I've heard that retirement can bring on depression. Have you talked to someone about this? Your doctor?" Jocelyn looked at him earnestly, reaching her hand over and resting it on his forearm.

"I don't get depressed." Mark said the words with confidence, but her expression was cynical.

"Oh, you're one of those guys. Too tough to ask for help?"

He sipped on his soda until it ran dry, his straw making an obnoxious noise. "Maybe I am one of those guys. I haven't needed to ask anyone for anything in a long time. And before that, there was never anyone to ask anyway. I just try to plow ahead. Fix on the next task. But there aren't any tasks right now."

"I bet what you're feeling is pretty common when people who have big careers retire. Especially people like us."

"Like us?" He eyed her closely, dying to know what she thought they had in common.

"People who knew we weren't destined for the usual path of forever marriages, children, and grandchildren. No one tells us what our twilight years are supposed to be like. The movies are all about the next generation. Being wise. Intrusively instilling them with our sage advice. Tinkering around the kitchen making recipes that span back generations in our family. Everyone knows that narrative. People like us, we have to make our own."

"Twilight years? I am not in my twilight years." He puffed out his chest. "I am in my prime. At most, the tail end of my prime."

"I knew that was going to be a trigger word." She slapped a hand to her thigh. "You men are all the same. Fragile little things, aren't you?"

"Very."

The movie was beginning to play and Mark turned the radio station to the channel that would produce the sound. It was static at first and then the singsong voices of the actors played.

Mark reclined his seat a bit and then looked over at Jocelyn. "I'm glad you came out tonight. This is fun."

She had a mouth full of cheese fries and was smiling with her eyes.

"We're not going in that back seat." She pointed a threatening finger at him. "You can forget about that."

"Jocelyn, I'm not that guy." He smiled and she blushed. "Plus I could break a hip trying to get back there. During these twilight years, I'm very fragile."

CHAPTER SEVEN

Gwen

The tall brick apartment building loomed overhead. It cast a shadow like a cartoon cloud that was comically following Gwen around while everyone else stood in the sun. A chill rolled up her back. Did anyone ever feel ready for these moments? Was it possible to be prepared for something like this?

Getting here had taken work. Flying cross-country. Renting the car. Locating the last known address of Markus Armand Ruiz. She and Griff had done a lot to bring them to this cracked sidewalk and crumbling front steps. The rusted medal handrail looked ready to bust out of the brick wall and the locked glass door was cloudy and covered in fingerprints. The first barrier to success came in the form of the building's security. They would need to be buzzed into the building by one of the tenants.

For some reason, she'd envisioned a different kind of home here. Nothing fancy. The way Leslie had described Mark made Gwen imagine a little ranch house with a few potted plants out front. Some shutters punctuating the sides of big bay windows. Maybe even an old dog asleep on the front porch. Something personal with character. This building was completely impersonal and nondescript.

"It's kind of a rough-looking place." Gwen rubbed her hands together nervously. "Leslie said he was a successful businessman. Why would he be living here?"

"That was twenty-seven years ago. A lot can change." Griff took a step back to appraise the building from another angle, as though it might look better. Gwen knew it wouldn't. This was a rundown apartment in a less-than-desirable part of the city. If he was living there then something wasn't adding up. Leslie had only given bits and pieces of the story about her time with Mark. She seemed guarded, as if it were a precious secret to hold on to. The little information she did provide had given Gwen a much different image of Mark and where he might be in the world now.

It wasn't as if she cared about how well-off Mark was or his station in life. People could get down on their luck. This was still her biological father. If he were having some kind of trouble, maybe her presence in his life could help.

"How long do you want to stand out here?" Griff stepped to her side and nudged her a little. "I think we should at least pretend to read the newspaper or something. We're lurking."

"We're not lurking, we're assessing." She glanced up again toward the top floor.

"I don't think there is any more to see."

"I'm going to ring the buzzer." She nodded but didn't take

a step forward. The unknown was paralyzing. That buzzer would be like the shot from a gun that started a race. She'd be swept up in the crowd, pulled forward by a tide of people. Once she did this, there would be no stopping. "I'm just not sure what I'm supposed to say. He doesn't have to buzz us in if he doesn't want to talk to me. Which means I somehow, over this tiny little speaker, have to compel him to care enough. Do I tell him I'm his daughter? Lay it all out there right away?"

"I'm not sure." Griff stepped forward and pressed the button.

"What are you doing? I'm not ready."

"I don't think the right answer is going to suddenly present itself to us. Let's just wait to see what he says." Griff rubbed her back and smiled.

"You pushed the buzzer." She pouted and narrowed her eyes at him.

"I did."

A voice, crackling with static called back. "Ah, who's this?"

"Hi," Gwen began, holding the button down with her thumb. She shot Griff an angry look. "My name is Gwen, and I was wondering if you had a minute to come down and talk."

There was a pause then the man's voice came back over the speaker. "Like about Jesus or something?"

Gwen's face twisted up with frustration. She was blowing it. "No, Mr. Ruiz. It's about me and how we might be related." She bit hard on her lip, trying to prevent the verbal vomit of over-explaining. The words were multiplying in her. Running out of room to be held back. Everything was at the tip of her tongue.

You slept with Leslie, who is my mother. She didn't tell you about me, but I exist and I don't know how you feel about that, but I'd like the opportunity to know you.

Another long pause from the man was followed by his hesitant and static-filled response. "I'm not Mr. Ruiz. That guy died."

A sharp blade pierced her chest and popped her lungs. She couldn't breathe. Her arm reached for Griff. He laced his fingers with hers urgently. He held tightly to save her from going under.

With his other hand he pressed the intercom button. "Mr. Ruiz died?" Griff asked. "When?"

The voice crackled again through the speaker. "I dunno. A couple of months ago I think. He went to the hospital and didn't come back. He used to live upstairs from me. When they evicted him or got rid of his stuff, or whatever, I took over his apartment. The plumbing in mine always sucked." The man's voice sounded too young to be Mark. Odds were he was telling the truth. Her father was dead. She'd missed her opportunity to know him by a couple of months.

"All right," Griff said, holding the button down. "Thanks for your time."

"Wait." The voice echoed around them as they stepped back. "Angela has some of his stuff if you want it. She couldn't keep it all but she tried to get like photographs and things she thought he wouldn't have wanted thrown away."

"Angela?" Griff asked, as he pulled Gwen in tighter to his side. "What apartment is she in?"

"Two-twenty. You can buzz her. She's home."

Griff moved his finger along the panel and found Angela's apartment number. Holding down the buzzer,

Gwen could feel he was holding his breath. It wasn't going to be much of a consolation prize getting a box of her father's things. The photographs would be nice to have but would they only highlight how much she'd missed. Maybe if she'd have worked harder to get more information on Mark, she could have found him sooner. Leslie had been right; Gwen had given up some of the spark and fight for a while. And in that time she'd lost him.

"He's dead?" Gwen asked, as though Griff could somehow offer her new information. "Recently? Like I just missed him?"

"Hello?" A woman's voice, rough-edged and impatient, coming through the speaker cut them off.

"Hi, Angela. My name is Griff. Your neighbor told us that you might have some belongings of Mr. Ruiz. I'm wondering if you have a minute to talk with us downstairs."

"I didn't steal that stuff," Angela replied bluntly. "It was all going to the trash. I just figured I'd hang on to some of the things that looked sentimental in case he got better. That's not a crime."

Griff nudged Gwen toward the button. She took the hint and got herself together. "Ma'am, I appreciate you keeping that stuff. It was thoughtful. We're not here because you're in any kind of trouble. I just have some questions about Mark."

"Markus, he went by Markus." The static crackled louder. "I can't come down right now. I'm busy." Angela sounded skeptical. As though she was sure there was trouble waiting for her out front. Gwen felt a pang of pain that neither she nor Leslie didn't know he went by Markus.

"Can you tell us when he died?" Griff asked, looking

determined to get as much information as he could before Angela inevitably sent them away. "How long ago?"

Angela made a strange noise, something between a gasp and a laugh. "He's not dead. Or he wasn't yesterday. He called to check on his fish. I took it that day the ambulance picked him up. I've been feeding it."

"Wait," Gwen lunged at the button and held it down with her thumb. "The guy who lives in his apartment now said Markus was dead."

"That kid wouldn't know. He was just waiting around for his apartment to free up. Markus is alive. But he's really sick. I don't think he's supposed to live too much longer. He told me to keep the fish. He wouldn't be back for it. He's at Saint Elvin's Hospice Care. You don't usually go there if they think you'll get better."

"Thank you," Gwen said. Sweat gathered on her palms and a tingle of nerves shot up her back. Her father had just suddenly died and then came back to life. All in the span of a minute or two. She took a couple steps away and then doubled back toward the intercom. "Angela. What's the name of his fish?"

There was a pause. "Hippo," she reported hesitantly.

Griff twisted his face up and gave Gwen a wild look. She wasn't sure if it was a reaction to her question, or the answer.

"He's not dead," Gwen breathed the words out as she moved back toward the street. "But he's dying."

"Why did you want to know the name of his fish?" Griff's expression told her he wasn't ready to let that slide. He had to walk fast to get back to her side.

"I think the name of a pet can tell you a lot about people.

Is their dog named Spot or Ezekiel Barkington III? That's important information."

"What does a fish named Hippo tell you?" His brows were raised high as though there would be nothing she could say to convince him how it was relevant.

Gwen ran her thumb over her chin contemplatively. "It means Mark is silly or ironic. He likes to tell a story. You name a fish Hippo and people are going to ask why. I'm just glad it's not named Fishy or Goldie or something literal and boring. That would have worried me."

"You have a strange process sometimes." Griff winked playfully. "Of all the things you could have asked Angela, I never would have come up with that one."

The tightness in her chest seeped back in. "What illness do you think he has? Maybe it's something genetic. Something I might be predisposed to." She put a hand to her head as though maybe a time bomb of a clot was just about to burst.

"Whoa, watch out horse, there goes the cart, way out front." He gestured animatedly as though something had just blown by them. "You have no idea why he's in the hospital, so don't get worked up."

"I'd refrain from calling me a horse, even as a fun expression. That'll get you kicked."

"Like with your hooves?" He snickered quietly and dodged the slap to his arm.

"There really is no bad time for a joke with you, is there?" Gwen tried to look angry but it was hard with Griff. He made even the toughest moments more bearable.

"Now is a great time for a joke. You just got good news. At least you came here in time," Griff offered calmly, trying to sound cheery about it. "That's a blessing. He's still alive. You have a chance to meet him."

Turning back toward their car, Gwen stopped abruptly, sending Griff bumping into the back of her. She couldn't shake the nerve-induced nausea plaguing her.

"What is it?" he asked. There was an anxious edge to his voice as his back went rigid. Ready to physically fight something off. Whatever stopped her in her tracks, he'd handle it.

Unfortunately, it was just her own worries that had slowed her down. "He's dying. People want peace when they're dying. They have to wrestle with all the different emotions that come with facing their mortality."

"You're right. It's probably a really difficult time for him." Griff leaned against the car and tucked his hands in his pockets. The haze of her worry lifted for just a second as she took him in. His casual stance and dimpled magazine-worthy smile. Maybe she was doing this all wrong. Maybe getting lost in him would feel endlessly better than all this push and pull of life she was doing. Would closing her eyes and jumping headlong into pleasure be better than scaling a wall, climbing toward the unknown?

"What?" Griff asked, looking down at himself, trying to see what she was staring at.

Shaking her head and dislodging the idea of instant gratification, she went on. "I don't intend to walk in and make it any more difficult for him. He's at the end of his life. He's gone this long without knowing about me. Now can't possibly be the right time to tell him." She was going to have to change her name to Waffle soon if she kept going back and forth like this. Uncertainty was constantly nipping at her heels now.

"From what Angela said, it sounds like this might be the only time you'll be able to tell him." Griff had earned the room to push Gwen. His argument could easily be blunter, more persuasive. He could even demand she take his advice, considering he'd flown her out here and arranged it all. But she could tell, he was giving her the space to get there on her own. All that space left her running back and forth in every direction. It wasn't fair; she wanted him to tell her what to do. If he decided at least she'd have someone to blame when it was all over.

"What if it upsets him? I don't want him to die angry because of me. I could leave things just the way they are right now." She cut her hands through the air as though it were decided, even though it obviously wasn't.

"You could do that." Griff looked down at his shoes and tapped one on the curb mindlessly.

"Stop that."

"Stop what?" He furrowed his brows and tossed a hand up defensively. "I'm being supportive."

"You're just agreeing with me. I know that's not how you really feel. You think what I'm saying is foolish and rooted in self-preservation. What you really think is, I'll regret it for the rest of my life if I don't go see him before he dies. The pain of not knowing will be far worse than any turmoil I create by visiting him. That's what you would do right? March in there, consequences be damned."

"No." He shook his head and softened his expression. That look usually meant he'd even table the jokes for a little while.

"I don't believe you. There is no way you'd just go back home and pretend you didn't find him? Let him die without ever meeting each other. You're trying some reverse psychology on me."

"No. I wouldn't do that either."

Her voice dropped from angry to pleading. "What would you do? Tell me what to do. My two options are to go in there and risk making things worse or go home and always wonder."

Griff ran a hand over his short dark hair and drew in a deep breath. His expression was pained. She knew he didn't like to see her suffering. And she'd been doing quite a lot of that since they reconnected. "I'm not here to decide all of this for you, Gwen. I can't. I don't know what it feels like to be standing out here. You're processing the news that your biological father is dying. That you might have a limited amount of time to decide what to do. I can't possibly tell you how you should handle that."

Taking a step closer, she closed the distance between them to less than a foot. The urge was there. She could reach out and put her hands on his sides. Brace herself there. But she didn't. Instead she let her eyes plead with him. "Then tell me how you would handle it if it were you."

"Me?" He pointed at his chest. "That's easy. I'd lie."

"To who?" She leaned back and gazed up at him quizzically.

"To Markus. I'd go see him in the hospital and pretend I was there for some other reason. A volunteer or something. I'd hold my cards close to my chest and figure out, after meeting him, whether or not I want to tell him the truth."

Her eyes went wide. "Lie?"

"Oh, come on, don't go all doe-eyed and sweet on me. Lying might make you squirm but in some circumstances it can spare some pain. We grew up very differently. Lying is another form of self-defense. You have to keep some things to yourself until you know it's safe to do otherwise. There's no harm in waiting for the right moment, or the right amount of information."

"Do you do that with me? What are the little white lies you tell to keep me happy?" Gwen crossed her arms over her chest, challenging him. Griff grew up in an emotional war zone. She could see how keeping things from his parents would be not only convenient but necessary. His idea actually made sense. There was a way to use the fact that Markus didn't know she existed in order to ease into the truth.

"No. I don't bother trying to sugarcoat things for you. We're past that." Griff shrugged and smiled his most adorable smile. His charm was blinding sometimes. If he didn't have a good heart, he'd be a very dangerous man.

"We're past that?" Her heart swam around her chest at that idea. The thought that they were so close that lies would be wasted between them.

"I could try to get one over on you, but lying to you wouldn't work. You know my signs. You'd pester me relentlessly until you got the truth. It would be exhausting. I wouldn't even bother."

"I do know when you're lying." She gloated proudly, pointing up at his face. "Your eyebrow twitches, and you always look to the left. I remember when my dad caught you trying to sneak nails out of his workshop. You tried to blame it on Dave. I thought your eyebrow would twitch right off your face."

"I felt awful about that. We were building some stupid raft to float down the creek. Your father had told us to stay away from there. There had been so much rain and the debris and current could have killed us. But we wanted to do it anyway."

"But he didn't bust you about the raft?"

"He knew we were building it, but he didn't say anything. The next day we went to the creek and the thing was gone. He either busted it all up or tossed it in the water. He let it slide though."

"He's good like that," Gwen said, gulping back her emotion. "I don't know how, but my dad's been so great about me coming out here. He keeps telling jokes and making it like it's no big deal. How can you raise and love someone for twenty-six years and not be at least a little worried when they go out searching for their biological parent? My mother, who is a saint, is jealous and nervous of what's to come. Did you see that party? That was all just her nerves about having Leslie and Kerry there. But my dad, he's been unflappable. I just worry that he's holding it all in, and it'll just bowl him over when he least expects it."

"Your dad is a tough guy, but he's also a very smart man. He knows you, and he knows the strong bond you two share. He's not faking it. I think he means what he's saying."

Gwen squinted playfully at him. "Are you lying now? I'm going to have to watch you very closely to make sure you mean what you say."

"I told you, there's no reason for me to bother trying to lie to you." He leaned in toward her, close enough to plant a kiss on her lips. Stopping and hovering there he whispered ominously, "So make sure you don't ask me any questions unless you want the truth."

CHAPTER EIGHT

Gwen

"Did you fill out the HIPAA paperwork online?" The nurse charging down the hall waved for them to keep up. Her thick-soled shoes squeaked as they turned a corner. She was built strong and sturdy, filling up her colorful scrubs with toned muscle. Gwen eyed her hair, spiked up with gel and dyed an unnatural shade of bleached blonde. Earrings, too many to count at this fast-walking pace, dotted up both her ears. A booming voice and big presence, this nurse was one of those women someone would describe as a character. Also not someone Gwen thought they should mess with. The idea of lying seemed dangerous.

Gwen opened her mouth to apologize about not having done the paperwork, but Griff spoke up first. "We sure did. Gosh, it's a lot of forms to deal with." He feigned disgust with the process.

Lying sent goose bumps up Gwen's arms. She'd always been terrible at it. Last year, keeping the secret of her miscarriage and her struggle to decide about sending her DNA off for testing was the hardest year of her life. It made her sick to cut out the people who loved her most. She'd made a promise to herself to do better. To feel better. Dr. Charmrose, her therapist, had given her plenty of techniques aimed at moving back to a space of openness and asking for help when she needed it. But lying to her biological father wasn't on that list. It made her stomach tighten. Even only lying by omission made her queasy.

"Bureaucracy," the nurse huffed, checking her watch and then looking back at them as she slowed down. "I'm buried in paperwork every day. More people would come in like you to volunteer if they didn't have so many hoops to jump through. I appreciate you putting in the effort and getting through the red tape."

"We didn't mind," Griff replied coolly. "It's worth it. People have so much to deal with in hospice care. If we can bring them even a little bit of joy it's worth it."

The nurse turned and eyed Gwen knowingly as she jutted her thumb out toward Griff. "Hold on to this one. Trust me, I've been around a lot longer than you. They don't make many men like him."

Gwen blushed and nodded. Griff was a great guy, but at the moment he was being a convincing liar. It was a dichotomy she wasn't used to with him.

"You can make your way through any of these rooms here. Just ask the patients if they are interested in some company. Renee," she said, waving her hand impatiently, "rooms two-thirteen and two-nineteen are nonresponsive, correct?"

"Yes," the rail-thin nurse said, shooting obediently to her feet. Her uniform hung too big on her as though it had been handed down. The rims of her large glasses rested on her cheeks and she pushed them up tighter to her tiny face. "They are sedated. Why?"

"We have some volunteers to visit and read to patients. Where do you think they should start?" The nurse was already fixated on the chart in her hand and half listening as Renee began to speak.

"Mr. Ruiz doesn't get any company at all. I would start in there." Renee rushed around the other side of the desk and tried to keep up when they began walking again. She was tiny, almost childlike in stature. Her voice came out like a squeak.

Gwen's heart sang at the sound of her father's name. He was here. This was happening. And their plan was working. As uneasy as it made her, Griff had been right. It was the best way to do this. Rushing in and announcing he was her father would have been too much. A little white lie would ease them all in.

Renee reported on Markus in a familiar kind of way that made Gwen wonder how long he'd been there. "Markus tells the best stories. When he's up to it, he can get the whole floor of nurses cackling over a joke he's told. He's a good man but he's very lonely. He doesn't have anyone at all who will come to see him." Renee looked pained by this.

"No family?" Griff asked, feigning empathy, which Gwen knew was his angle of gathering information.

On the ride over they had talked about how important it

would be to get a sense of who Markus is. They should try to understand him and his life before he had the chance to shut down and keep things from them.

Renee hummed and looked down at her shoes. "It's a complicated situation." When the first nurse with the spiky hair rounded a corner and disappeared, Renee began to explain further. She looked liberated by their sudden privacy. "I try to spend some of my extra time in there with him. He really likes to play cards. I brought a radio in from home and he likes to listen to the baseball games on it. No one should have to be that alone in the end. It's a tragedy."

Gwen took in Renee's sweet eyes and thin angelic face. They were probably around the same age, but Renee could pass for a teenager. Her long brown hair sat in a braid over her shoulder and her thick bangs danced just above her eyelashes. She was cute as a button, but looked too sad for her own good. Gwen felt compelled to know more. Who was this woman who was being so kind to Markus? "Do you do that for all your patients?"

"Most patients, when they reach hospice care, are surrounded by their loved ones. Even if they didn't have the best relationships to begin with, they still come. Or it's friends from work. People they've known for years. In this stage of illness most can move past that old hurt and find a way to make peace. People understand there isn't much time left, and they say what needs to be said. For Mr. Ruiz, no one has come."

"How long does he have?" Griff asked, as they slowed down their stride and got to another set of rooms.

Renee looked suddenly self-conscious. "I really shouldn't discuss his prognosis with anyone. I'm just glad he'll have some company. It would be great if you could come and see him now and then." She lowered her voice. "For the next couple of weeks."

Weeks.

That was the answer. The disgusting bad luck of it all. Gwen would find her father and have him for, at most, a couple of weeks. Fourteen days? If she'd have put this trip off, she could have lost him before ever connecting. But now she'd have him and have to let him go. It all felt heavy.

"We'll try to see him again," Griff said through a smile. "Thank you for your help, Renee. We'll come see you on our way out."

"Please do." She beamed as she entered the room and swept the curtain to the side with a swoosh of her arm. "Mr. Ruiz, I have some great news. You've got some company. These two would like to spend some time visiting if that's all right with you."

The man lying in the bed was frail in a way Gwen had never seen before in person. His collarbones were like razors, looking ready to cut through his paper-thin skin. The pale gray of his eyes looked nearly vacant, sunken deep into his tired face. His hair was mostly gone, just a few tufts shooting up from odd spots on his discolored scalp. His skin was spotted by too much time in the sun.

Renee checked a few of the machines around him and then patted his hand gently. "You have a nice visit. I'll be by later. Maybe tell them that story about the Dodgers game where you caught that foul ball."

Gwen pinched the back of Griff's arm and drew his eyes to hers. There would be no tactful way to say what needed to be said. The words clawed at the back of her throat. She wanted to yell them. But she stopped herself.

He's too old.

Griff didn't wait for her to pinch him again. "I know," he whispered as he pulled two chairs together near the foot of the man's bed.

"Hi, Mr. Ruiz," Gwen said, in a singsong voice she hardly recognized. It was fake and forced. Judging by the unimpressed look on the man's face, he could tell. "I hope you don't mind some company."

They both sat tentatively and she saw Griff stifle a smirk. They'd done all this only to find out they were incorrect. Sitting down next to the wrong man for a visit. This was what lying got you. Karma. Griff looked as though he were reading her mind as he cleared his throat and tried to make the best of it. "Yeah, we'd love to hear that story about the Dodgers game. Do you mind, Mr. Ruiz?"

Markus Ruiz, the wrong Markus Ruiz, tried to sit up a bit. He failed and instead just turned his head toward them. "Call me Markus." He sounded abundantly annoyed. "I don't want to talk about that game."

"All right, Markus," Griff continued. "We can talk about whatever you want."

Markus coughed but didn't bother, or wasn't able, to raise his hand up toward his mouth. "Why?"

"Why what?" Gwen asked, her smile unnaturally big. Her feelings were moving in a tight cyclone through her insides. This was Markus Armand Ruiz. This was supposed to be her father. But it couldn't be. According to Leslie, there had been an age difference between them. She had thought that at most he was ten years older than her. This man looked like he was in his eighties. She was disappointed for running this far down the wrong path, but also felt for the man in the bed. He was their only company, and they had no real reason to be there.

Markus ran his tongue over his dry lips and winced at some pain in his arm. "Why are you here? A couple of good-looking kids like you should be out partying, having a good time. Is this court-ordered or something? Some kind of community service?"

Griff chuckled. "Maybe we're just a couple of good people trying to spread our cheery dispositions and joy wherever we can."

"Right," Markus scoffed, and then coughed and gasped. "Sell that bull somewhere else. I've been around the block enough times to know everyone has an agenda. An angle they're working. I spent too many years trying to pull stuff like this to be fooled now. If you're thinking this dying old man has some fortune to hand out, you're mistaken." His cough erupted again, this time lingering as he tried to draw in breath.

"Are you all right?" Gwen asked, looking to the door as if she should go back and get Renee.

"I'm fine. Stop looking so worried. I'm already dying. You can't make it any worse. You're welcome to stay, but I've got to know why. Some church thing? I'm not religious. Maybe next week I will be. When I'm really close to the end I might decide to be safe rather than sorry. But this week, I'm still an atheist."

Gwen felt sorry for this guy. He wasn't her father and it had been a disappointing dead end, but it was hard to sit in the presence of someone who knew they were going to die.

Time felt endless for her. She was the age of feeling invincible. Gwen understood life could be fragile, but there seemed to be enough time. Time to screw up and make it right. Time to see where things went with Griff. Enough minutes and hours and years to tell her brothers she loved them or her parents how proud she was to be their daughter. She couldn't imagine all the things she'd try to do and say, if she only had a couple of weeks to live. "We're really just here to visit."

"Because?" Markus narrowed his eyes and pursed his thin, wrinkle-rimmed lips. "If it's a secret don't worry, I'm a great person to confide in. I'll take it to my grave. Pretty soon actually." He smiled a row of crooked teeth at them and closed his eyes for a long beat.

Gwen's mind wandered as she considered what all this meant to her story now. Was her father alive and well? Had he died of something else years ago? They'd be back at square one. Maybe he'd moved to another country. The idea that he'd stayed in California was a long shot. Her eyes roamed toward the window as she wiped a tear from her cheek.

"What's wrong with her?" Markus asked Griff, his throaty voice startling Gwen back to the moment.

"I'm fine, sorry." She straightened her back and crossed her legs. "Did you want to talk about that Dodgers game?"

"I never went to a Dodgers game." He snickered and his eyes showed a hint of mischief. "But Renee comes around here every day trying to make me feel better. She wants to hear how well I lived my life. How good it all was. Young people, they want to believe that a long life means a good life. It's impossible for sweet Renee to imagine my family wouldn't come here to see me. Or that I squandered away years upon years chasing something I would never find. I tell her the stories to make her feel better. She's a little obsessed with me."

"You have family?" Gwen asked, conjuring up images of her own clan. There would be nothing in the world to keep her from the bedside of any of them. The Fox family showed up, even when things weren't perfect.

"Relations by blood, sure. I've got plenty of them. But they haven't considered me family for a long time. They won't be coming around here. I'm good with that. No skin off my back. I tried to tell Renee that, but she keeps writing them letters and calling them." He laughed humorlessly, cringing a bit at the pain. "There would be nothing in the world she could write or say that would change any hearts or minds. But she doesn't believe me."

Griff eyed Gwen and asked the question before she could. "Renee is writing them letters asking them to come visit you?"

Markus's overgrown gray eyebrows knit together, making him look worried suddenly.

"Don't say anything to the other nurses or anyone. She'd probably get in trouble for it. I don't have the heart to tell her some bridges burned to ash. You can't rebuild them. In a couple weeks I'll be dead, and she'll be fine."

"I'm sorry they don't want to see you." Gwen's eyes filled with tears but she blinked them away. Her life was full to the brim with emotional quandaries. She certainly couldn't go around taking in anyone else's problems.

"Oh, don't you start too." Markus scolded her. His gravelly voice was getting weaker the longer they stayed. He jutted his chin toward the plastic pitcher of water and tiny cup. Griff rose to fill it and handed it over. Markus didn't bother with a thank you. "Don't be sorry for me. Be sorry for them. My kids had a dad not worth knowing. Even when he's dying." He turned his head toward the window and closed his eyes.

"Maybe they'll answer one of her letters," Gwen offered gently. "You never know what people will do. I showed up out of the blue and met my biological mother. I wasn't sure what would happen, but it's been good so far."

Markus nodded but clearly only to appease her. "I'm not sure what kind of visit this might be. I don't really have any great stories, and I don't have the energy to make up the ones I do for Renee."

Griff looked at Gwen and then shifted his eyes toward the door. She shook her head. Leaving now felt cruel. They'd only been there a short time, and now that they knew no one else was coming to visit, it seemed wrong to get up and leave. She leaned in a bit. "You must have one good story. Something you remember fondly. It doesn't have to be movie worthy, just something that makes you smile. You don't even have to embellish for us. It can be boring."

Markus sneered and looked to Griff. "What's with all these sweet girls? They really do think we're better than we are."

Griff grinned and planted his hand on Gwen's knee. "And thank God for that. Someone needs to believe we're worth putting up with."

Markus pulled the thin hospital blanket up higher and shivered a bit. "The only good things in life I remember are from before."

"Before what?" Gwen asked, wondering how hard it could be to remember a morsel of happiness in more than eighty years of life. She'd lived a fraction of that and could easily recall moments of pure joy. Maybe that made her lucky.

Markus cleared his throat. "Before I threw my life away. Before I left for that gallon of milk and never went back home. There's this thing." He looked contemplatively at the ceiling, seeming to search for the words that they, as young people, could understand. "It's a siren song that calls people and convinces them there's something better out there. A better life. A better job. A better woman. I listened to that song. I walked away from my family and I never looked back. I spent years chasing the idea that I could do better. But it's like getting to the end of a rainbow. It's all an illusion. The pot of gold was never there to begin with."

Gwen's stomach went sour. What kind of person could abandon their family just because they thought they could do better? She kept hunting for redeeming qualities in Markus, other than a terminal disease, that might make him worthy of sympathy. She hung on every word, rooting around in the conversation like a pig searching determinedly for truffles. But the more he talked the less she found.

"My parents are no model citizens either," Griff interjected. "But if they were dying I'd show up. Either for me to have some peace or for them to at least believe I'd found some. Maybe instead of Renee pleading your case, you should. Maybe it would mean more to your kids if the letter came from you."

Markus rolled his eyes. Even that small motion seemed to take a lot out of him. "Aren't you two supposed to read me a book or something? Play me music from when I was young? Because I'm not here to be preached to. I didn't ask Renee to write those letters. I think the best gift I could give my kids is dying without them ever having to see me. Every story needs a villain, and I'm all right being theirs. Let them hate me. Everyone has to hate someone."

"Is that a rule?" Gwen asked, shooting him a look to show she was unimpressed by his deflection. Markus was putting on a tough face but she could see it around the edges of his sunken eyes. No one wanted to die alone. Even if they believed they deserved to.

"It should be a rule." He set his bony jaw tightly. "I'm tired. I need to rest."

Gwen hummed disapprovingly as he closed his eyes and pretended he was nearly asleep. "But if you just—"

Griff's hand touched her on the back gently as he stood. "Come on. We need to go."

Standing, she looked down at Markus. She was struck suddenly by the revelation that she was glad this man wasn't her father. Glad she didn't have to board the crazy roller coaster of meeting him and then mourning him. It was a completely inappropriate time to relish relief, but she couldn't avoid it. This felt like a dodged bullet.

When Griff and Gwen stepped into the hallway she rested a hand on the wall, steadying herself. "Obviously he's not my father."

"I still feel for the guy. I'm sure we all get to the end of our lives and have some regrets. He's got nothing but regrets. That's tough."

Renee peeked around the corner suddenly, shuffling her way toward them. "Out already?"

They both jumped a bit at the sound of her voice. "He was tired," Griff reported. "We thought he better just rest."

Renee fidgeted with the clipboard in her hands. "If you two could just keep it to yourself about me trying to contact his family that would be great. I've blurred the lines a bit between what's kind and what's ethical. I really thought if they knew, they'd come."

"How many children does he have?" Griff asked.

"Four." She quieted as two other nurses passed and then started again when they were out of earshot. "But I've only been able to find two. One of his daughters kept her maiden name. The other two must not have so I didn't have any luck with tracking them down. And his son was easy to find, obviously."

Griff seemed to perk up. "Obviously?"

"He's Markus Armand Ruiz Junior so I didn't have much trouble tracking him down. Though he only goes by Mark. He actually only lives a couple hours from here whereas the daughter lives on the East Coast. I figured if any of them would come it would be his son. I wrote him like five letters. Left a couple voice mails. I just wanted him to know how urgent it was."

Gwen offered a kind smile. "I can tell you care a lot. I promise we won't say anything to anyone."

"Going to see his son in person would be too much, right?" Renee's lashes fluttered and she held her breath. Her cheeks flushed and her eyes darted away.

"Yeah," Griff said rather sharply. "It sounds like you could find yourself on thin ice if you did that. You're so nice, but I don't want to see you get in trouble. Gwen and I could go instead."

"We could." Gwen nodded her agreement. She and Griff were in sync. Obviously this man's son could be her father.

The age worked out. Now it would just be a matter of getting the right information.

"It's obviously very important to you, Renee," Griff said, using a voice Gwen could spot as disingenuous. "And after spending just a little time with Markus, it's clear he does want to see his children."

Gwen felt like they were all doing this delicate dance of deception. Renee had a responsibility to her role as a caregiver. She couldn't cross the line anymore than she already had.

"Gwen and I were so touched by your dedication." Griff put a hand over his heart. "I honestly don't know how you do this job. It takes a very special kind of person."

"Thank you. I actually have to get back to my other patients. You two have been great. If you are able to track Markus Junior down I hope you can convince him to come by." Renee beamed as she laid Markus's folder on her desk. "I think if you find him and convey to his son just how serious Markus's illness is and how little time he has left, he'd come by."

Griff nodded his agreement. "Have a good rest-of-your-shift. I completely understand. We'll do our best."

It wasn't until they were alone that he leaned over the desk and flipped the folder open.

"What are you doing?" Gwen scolded in a hushed voice. "We can't go through his record."

"Why do you think Renee left it here?" Griff shot back, taking his phone out and snapping a quick picture. "It has his son's contact information in here."

"Markus didn't seem like he wanted to see his kids. He was pretty clear. Renee wasn't acting on his behalf. Maybe we should leave all of this alone. It feels like we're playing with fire."

Griff turned the phone toward her and smiled. "Mark Armand Ruiz Junior is probably your father. The age, as Markus's son, would work out right. We didn't get many other hits on the name out here. This is our best lead and we didn't even have to try to dig up the address. It was right here for the taking. I call that a win."

She took in the information a few gulps at a time, like she was chugging down something warm and unpalatable. In theory it made sense, but the reality was less appealing. If Griff was right, that would make the man they just met, the man dying in hospice care, her grandfather. It would mean her biological father had managed to receive letters and voice mails that should have compelled him to be there and he didn't bother to oblige. All the relief she felt about Markus not being her relative evaporated like morning dew under the hot sun. What kind of man would not visit his dying father?

The idea of going home right now without knowing for sure was appealing. But she knew better. Not knowing was like an aggressive cancer. She had to face this now.

"So we go find him?" Gwen asked, gesturing to Mark's address. "And do we lie again when we get there?"

"Yes." Griff grinned and tucked the address away. "I think we're getting rather good at it."

CHAPTER NINE

Mark

Even daydreaming of his night out with Jocelyn hadn't been enough to distract him when another letter arrived. He recognized the familiar bubbly lettering the moment he pulled it from the mailbox. Tossing it down on the kitchen table he wondered if maybe he was overreacting. It was just a letter from someone trying diligently to change his mind. That took determination and resolve, characteristics he usually admired in people. Yet, all he felt was bothered. Intruded upon.

Mark appreciated persistence, but it was becoming disruptive. He'd obviously, by not responding, given this nurse his answer. He had no intention of going to see his father. The man hadn't even bothered to write a letter himself. He instead somehow tricked this kind nurse into taking up his cause. Manipulation was very on-brand for his father.

It was laughable to think that now, just because death was involved, Mark should want to see him. The two had zero communication for decades. No relationship in life, so therefore no need for one as his father transitioned to death. Perhaps this campaign to fix their relationship would have been more effective if it weren't born out of desperation.

It had been a few weeks since he'd checked in with his sisters. This should have warranted a call to them. Were they getting the same letters and phone calls? His curiosity was not powerful enough to step on that slippery slope. What if they had gotten the letters and decided to see him? There was a chance they'd pressure him to do the same.

Their father was a taboo subject in the family. If there were any fond memories from before he left, they'd all decided not to discuss them. If there was resentment for his leaving, they'd buried that as well. It had been as though he never existed and everyone seemed satisfied to leave it that way.

This time he didn't bother opening the letter. Renee seemed painfully sweet and sincere. It was impossible to believe she had any hidden motivation. She was just another victim of his father. His charisma was blinding, and Renee seemed like the perfect target. Youthful. Kind. And unfortunately, a sucker.

He ripped the envelope into small pieces and tossed it in the trash. Eventually the letters would stop, because eventually his ailing father would die. There would be no reason for Renee to plead for him then. His anger couldn't be directed at Renee, but there was plenty of it set aside for his father. He seethed with frustration.

With annoyance still pulsing through his body, he turned

abruptly out of the kitchen, catching his foot hard on the doorframe. Pain shot like lightning bolts from his toes up his leg. This was his bad foot. It used to act up a bit when he'd go play racquetball, but now that he was retired it only took a little tweak or a looming rainstorm to start bothering him. Kicking the wall surely did some damage.

Mark hobbled to the couch and shouted some of the more obscene curse words he knew. His foot throbbed, and he was sure at least two of the toes were broken. This would kill his golf game. Tennis with Jocelyn would be out.

Is this how it starts?

Did the injuries begin piling up until the only thing he could do was wheel himself next to a bay window and watch the birds flapping around?

Doubling back to the kitchen for ice, he fought the urge to kick the wall out of spite. *That will teach it to get in my way again.*

He knew well enough that wouldn't help. And the wall wasn't to blame. If he hadn't been so damn upset about this nurse hounding him he wouldn't have been slamming around the house so quickly. Mark could practically hear the jokes from his pals already. They'd be offering to pay for his life-alert system, so he could just push a button if he fell and couldn't get up.

His mind spun with everything this injury could cause. Would he need a cast? Could he still drive? It was a disaster.

When the doorbell rang he realized it was the first time he'd heard it since moving in. Everyone he'd invited over had known to knock on the side door. The front door was closer to the driveway, but he'd used the entryway behind it to store his sports equipment. It wasn't easy to get around it. No one had popped in unexpectedly. The house was set back on the far side of the lake. The dirt road was only wide enough for one car and there were no signs that would direct someone right to his place. Even GPS didn't do that well at getting people to the correct spot.

Mark shuffled angrily toward the front door and edged by his golf clubs and bike. When his shirt caught on his bike handle he yanked it free, the bike toppling over and crashing to the ground, almost hitting his injured foot. It wedged itself awkwardly between the door and the wall, making it even harder to answer the ringing doorbell.

"What?" he yelled, bending down to try to right his bike.

"Mr. Ruiz?" The woman's voice was tentative but loud enough to carry through the closed door.

"I don't use the front door. I have stuff back here." Mark slammed the bike back against the wall, the reflector smashing. "Damn it. What do you want?"

"Sir," a man's voice interjected, and Mark reached a hand to one of his golf clubs. Would anyone come out all this way to rob him? It was certainly a quiet enough place to get away with something.

When the man started talking again, Mark slid one club out and clutched it. "My name is Griff. We just want to talk to you for a minute. Should we go to the side door?"

"Yeah, fine. Go to the side door." Mark looked down at his foot. It was beginning to swell. Whoever this was had better have a good reason for being here. The throbbing in his foot was nothing compared to the pulsing of his adrenaline.

Mark wasn't historically quick to anger. He'd never been accused of having a bad temper. But things were different lately. Everything was out of sorts. Backward. Maybe the only reason he was good at keeping himself calm before was because he didn't want to deal with Human Resources or a bad reputation in business. Now he was some retired guy who could be as cranky as he wanted to be. Clichés must be there for a reason. Never did he think he'd be the guy who shook his fist and told those kids to get off his lawn. But that was coming.

Hobbling toward the side door he braced himself against the furniture and walls. With the other hand he used the golf club like a cane.

"Are you all right?" the girl's voice floated through the screen door. Their eyes were on him, faces washed with concern.

"I'm fine. What can I do for you?" He straightened up quickly, not wanting to look like an easy target if they were here to give him trouble. He flipped the golf club up onto his shoulder and held it like a bat, casually resting it but ready to swing if he needed to.

"Like I said, my name is Griff. We were at the Saint Elvin's Hospice Care Center earlier today."

No. This was impossible. There was no way the facility where his father had gone to die had actually sent people to his house. There had to be some kind of law against that. The nerve they had was astounding.

"Go." He pointed to where their car was parked. "I've received plenty of correspondence already about this. I do not wish to see him. Leave me alone."

The girl leaned back as though his words had wounded her. As if this was personal. Long slow blinks of her lashes were like judgmental barbs at his soul. He didn't need it. "Listen, Renee, I am sure you are a lovely girl. But my father is using you. That's what he does. He's very charming. Oodles of charisma. The stories he tells are always very elaborate, easy to get caught up in. I'm not blaming you."

Her mouth dropped open suddenly. "Mr. Ruiz, I'm not—"

"I don't care." He lowered the golf club from his shoulder and it made a loud thud on the wood floor. "I don't care about him. I don't care what he wants or needs. That man is a stranger to me. And trust me, no matter what he tells you, he's a stranger to you too. The best advice I can give you is to keep your distance."

Griff cleared his throat. "He's dying. I can assure you, he's too frail to be a danger to anyone."

"My father's superpowers were never about size or strength. As long as he can speak he can hurt people. Now please, go." He pointed again to their car. "If anyone comes back here or approaches me again about this, you'll hear from my lawyer. This is completely inappropriate, and I'm sure you both know that."

"I'm sorry we bothered you," she said, wiping a tear from her cheek. "We won't be back."

Mark stepped through the screen door, leaning against it, and watched them walk back to their car. The girl's shoulders shook with the crash of emotions. Damn his father for laying his burden on this young woman. For bringing her to tears over a man she didn't know. A man who wasn't worthy of a single tear, let alone all the ones he saw streaming down her face as the car pulled away. He'd given up crying over that man decades ago. He wished everyone else would too.

The throbbing in his foot grew unbearable as he looked down at the skin starting to bruise. The only thing that hurt worse was the bursts of guilt in his gut. No matter how he felt about his father and the intrusion of unexpected company and his pounding foot, it didn't justify how he'd acted. Running them off was a jerk move. Those two kids didn't need to be yelled at. That poor girl, reduced to tears.

Getting himself to the couch he elevated his foot and grunted angrily at his current situation. A broken body. A short temper. His past trying to bust through the walls he'd created. This was not the retirement he'd imagined. When his phone rang he realized he'd left it on the counter in the kitchen. Out of reach. Instead of limping back to get it, he rested his head on the arm of the couch and closed his eyes. It would go to voice mail. It wouldn't be important anyway. Hardly anything was anymore.

CHAPTER TEN

Gwen

She was too lucky. That was the problem. Gwen hadn't suffered enough in her life. There had been so few letdowns. She'd had a middle-class upbringing with two amazing parents at the helm of the ship. Protective and loving brothers. Good friends. Access to a wonderful education.

Her breakup with Ryan and sudden miscarriage had been devastating, but even then, she'd had support. All of that love left her unprepared for this disappointment. The utter shock of her interaction with Mark still had her reeling.

"Leslie said he was one of the best men she'd ever known," Gwen sputtered out. "That not a nice man. Maybe it's the wrong Mark. We don't know for sure really."

Griff drove down the long flat road, keeping his eyes fixed forward. He was obviously trying to let her vent, get it all out, before he said anything. But there was very little left to say.

Instead, she leaned forward to catch his eyes and gave him a look as if she thought he weren't listening.

Griff nodded. "I think it was the right Mark. There was quite a resemblance. Or I thought so anyway."

"Yeah," she sighed, slapping her hands down to her thighs. "I saw it too. Damn. I really believed what Leslie said. I had this image of him. Some jolly old man with a charming smile. She said he changed her life. The way she described his demeanor and empathy sounded almost too good to be true. I was going to be the surprise he never saw coming. A good surprise. Now I never want to see him again."

"We left without telling him." Griff tightened his hands on the wheel, readying for her argument. "He doesn't have enough information to know how he feels about you."

"Are you serious?" She arched her brows up high. "I wouldn't want that man in my life no matter what. He's a jerk. Yelling at us, kicking us out. He won't even go see his dying father. I wouldn't give him the satisfaction of the truth. He doesn't deserve it."

"We were there under false pretenses, and he was reacting to that." Griff's voice was soft as if he knew he'd have to compensate for the yelling she was about to do.

She made an exasperated grunting noise. "That was your idea. You were on Team Liar. I just went along with it."

"I know. I think it's a good way to get your foot in the door, but what you do once you are there is important too."

"He kicked us out." She gestured back in the direction of Mark's house. It wasn't as if they'd had time to explain anything. He was a jerk right out of the gate. The sour taste in her mouth was hard to swallow down.

"If you'd have told him right then, he might have reacted

differently." Griff looked stiff, ready for a slap to his arm or at least an aggressive talking to. She loved that he put himself in that position. He was unafraid of the backlash that came from being real with her.

Gwen clenched her hands together tightly, fighting the urge to bang them on the dashboard. Why did Mark have to be a jerk? "No way. I don't care if he would have suddenly been nicer because he knew I wasn't Renee. Knowing he would have been mean to her is enough for me. He's not worth my time. I'm done with that."

"You're done with it?" Griff looked skeptical. "You're done with trying to connect to your biological father?"

"I'm sorry we came all this way for nothing. At least now I know what kind of man I come from. I should be glad he didn't raise me. I'd probably be an ass too." Gwen rested her head against the window and sulked. Knowingly stuck her lip out and pouted.

"He might be having a bad day. He looked like he hurt his foot or something. You never know what people are going through. Plus we showed up out of the blue. We might have startled him."

"I don't care. That's not how I wanted it to happen. I'm just going to have to move on. We should go back home."

Griff drew in a deep breath. "No, we should take some time to think about all this. We just got here. And he's not the only person you're related to. You have a grandfather here. One who's terminally ill and has no company at all. That's something to consider."

Gwen wanted to fire back another frustrated quip. But like usual Griff's words forced her to think. That was her grandfather lying in that bed. He was dying alone. Maybe this was the real reason she was out there. Perhaps she'd been put in his path to bring him some kind of peace. "I don't know if he'd even want me there," she worried aloud. "He didn't seem that receptive to it."

"He thought we were two strangers coming to convert him or something. If he knew you were family, maybe that would change his mind. I know it's a risk. No one wants to be rejected, and you'd be putting yourself in a position where that might happen. But remember what your grandfather said in the hospital. He's a great person to share a secret with. You could tell him."

"I could." She softened to the idea like dry soil under a heavy rain. "What if I find out I'm from a long line of jerks?" She eyed him, waiting for his joke. Ready to cut back with her own when he dared to say it.

"That's a trap. I'm not walking into that one." He shook his head vigorously. "Why don't we sleep on it and you can decide in the morning?"

"We've got a fancy hotel? Something on the beach, right?"

"No." He chuckled and wagged a finger at her. "We've got an economy room with two beds in a decent area, nowhere near the beach. I'd like to save at least some of my travel points for a vacation that doesn't involve your drama."

"Feel free to take any of your other lady friends wherever you like. I am not the one who booked this and insisted we come." Sparks of nervousness rolled up her arms. It was a strange position to be in. She was not in a relationship with Griff, but she desperately hoped no one else would be either. It was a space she couldn't fill but wanted it to stay open. Aware of how selfish that seemed, she promised herself she would do better. It wasn't fair to him. Before she could resign herself to losing him to someone else he swooped in and assured her she had nothing to worry about.

"You need to listen more closely. I said I hoped my next vacation wouldn't include your drama. I want all my vacations to include you. I'll take you on a nice trip someday. We'll lie on the beach and drink fruity drinks. We'll swim in tropical blue water and forget what day it is."

For the sake of her own heart, she felt compelled to temper his words with reality. "Griff, don't you think we make a lot of promises to each other we can't keep? Life is going to come along and we'll both get swept up in it. We've barely seen each other in the last few months. If we were actually going to do something we would have by now."

Gwen didn't want to sound desperate. The phone worked both ways, and she hadn't called him much either. It wasn't that she hadn't wanted to call him. There wasn't a night that went by where she didn't long to hear his voice. But there had been less to say each passing day. They'd check in with each other, but if they weren't going to take it to the next level then there was only so much to talk about. And neither one of them seemed brave enough to take the leap. They knew they were standing at the edge of something and once they started there would be no stopping. With all that had happened it seemed impossible to take the risk.

Griff looked at her for a beat. "Running into you over the holidays was intense. Going off together and digging into your past was not something I'd planned. When it was all done and you went back to school, I realized I had better take some time to think about things. Figure out what was left when the intensity of what we were doing was gone."

She gulped, afraid of his answer. "I felt the same way. How much of what we were feeling was just adrenaline and circumstances?"

"That's what I was wondering too." He took her hand in his.

"And so, you thought about it, right?" Gwen couldn't read his expression. Was he about to break her heart or profess his love? She wasn't really ready for either.

"I started to think about it," he admitted. "I tried to separate all the things we were doing from how I was feeling. What would have happened between us if I came home for Christmas and saw you a couple of times. If some of this other stuff hadn't happened you'd probably still be with Ryan."

Gwen had been thinking about that a lot lately. Therapy had that effect on her. If she hadn't lost their child, she and Ryan could very well be married by now. Raising the baby. Maybe even living there in California where he'd come to start his company. Things between them before the sudden and devastating miscarriage hadn't been bad. Maybe it wasn't all sparks and lightning bolts, but that was to be expected for two school-minded people with a lot on their plate. Her therapist, Dr. Charmrose, had cautioned against endless what-if scenarios. There was no point. But when it came to moving forward, it was only fair to acknowledge the circumstances that had catapulted her life in a completely new direction.

"I'm not sure exactly where Ryan and I would be in our lives if I hadn't lost the baby. That was what started my path to find my biological family."

"Maybe it's something you need to think more about before you move on to anything else. If it was only circumstances that broke you up, maybe under the right circumstances you would be back together."

Gwen would be lying if she said she hadn't thought of that as well. But Ryan was in a new relationship now as far as she knew. And too much time had passed. Too many things, including her, had changed. "I have no problem moving on from Ryan. That's not the issue."

"But there is an issue?"

"I don't know. Every time I think we should get on with it already, I convince myself it's not the right time. There has to be a reason I'm hesitating." She felt as though she were standing on the edge of a cliff waiting for him to pull her back. "And so what did you come up with during all those months of thinking?"

"Don't be mad." He winced preemptively.

"Just spit it out."

"No, I mean don't be mad that I'm not sure. I don't have an answer either. I'm usually a very decisive person. I see something I want and I go for it. That's how I've always been. But losing my job rattled me, and now I'm in this holding pattern. More of a think it out then wait and see. It's got nothing to do with you. I actually went to your graduation party with the intention of laying it all out there. Things had settled down so you and I could actually find a way to make our schedules and commutes work. I got pretty far down the path of planning it all. There was a PowerPoint presentation. Graphs and stuff."

"What kind of graphs?" she asked, blinking hard at him.

"Some pie charts regarding how we could effectively split our time. Line charts that show the risk versus reward of starting a relationship. It was very well thought out. I had a thirty-, sixty-, and ninety-day check-in for us to see how things were going."

"This sounds so sexy, I'm not sure I can contain myself."

"Trust me," he said, pumping his hands in the air like he was slowing her down. "If you'd have seen the killer graphics I used, you wouldn't have been able to keep your hands off me."

"But you didn't show me any of it?" Gwen tried to keep her face soft and unaffected. Griff wasn't trying to hurt her. To the contrary, he was always trying to help her.

"You hit me with the news about your dad and I took it as a sign. I know that there's no perfect time to start a relationship. The presentation was just kind of a funny way of telling you I've really given it a lot of thought. But I do think there are times in life that don't set us up for success.

"You need a friend right now. Not some shiny new relationship to get lost in. And when we do finally get home and settled, I want you to really feel like you're ready to take a chance on us. It can't be because you're hurting or scared or confused. Those are all things you should be feeling in your life right now. When you get on solid ground, I'll be there either way. We'll just maybe make out more."

She laughed. "I really want to see those charts. You always seem to come up with the right answers to everything."

"Just hold up a second. I don't want you to think I'm being chivalrous and trying to protect your heart. There's a good part of my thinking that's self-preservation. There is no doubt in my mind how I feel about you. I'm all in and the idea of us blowing this terrifies me. I feel like we're going to have a shot at something great, but we need to take that shot when it's right."

"So it's just another road trip to find one of my parents. It's like last time. We sleep in the hotel room. Act like roommates?"

"It's an exercise in immense willpower for me." He groaned and kicked his head back. "But the good news is, you will be out of parents to search for after this. Work starts. You unpack at the house. I didn't tell you about the chart that covers sleepovers. The data points are pretty amazing."

"Were you always a nerd and I didn't notice?" She leaned back and pretended to scrutinize him. "Because I had no idea."

"Yeah, these long lashes and the dimple usually make the girls swoon too much to notice that I'm a geek. Plus you've had a thing for me for so long you were more interested in writing my name in your notebooks than checking my grades."

"Hmm." She tapped her chin. "I'm seeing you in a new light suddenly. Something to consider."

"Oh please, I can bench press you and do your taxes, I don't see how you'll keep your hands off me."

"I'll manage."

CHAPTER ELEVEN

Gwen

Waking up in a hotel with Griff again was as good as she remembered it. Maybe better. This time she was far more aware of her attraction to him. They weren't dancing around the idea that they wanted each other. She knew how he felt about her, and it made the atmosphere in the room completely different. It felt like a test run. What would their relationship really be like?

Having him close was comforting. Putting on a sweatshirt that smelled like him made her feel like a girl pining after her school crush. Which coincidentally he had been. When they moved past each other they would share a playful touch or tickle. Their jokes were layered with innuendo and teasing that she hoped, no matter what happened between them, would never end.

It was a dangerously flirtatious dance but one they both

seemed engaged in. It wasn't until real life crept back in that Gwen would deflate. And that was the point they'd both been trying so hard to make. The hotel rooms and the long car rides were fun and easy. Being in each other's company for those moments made perfect sense.

It was when she was marching blindly toward the unknown that she worried about loving Griff. How could there be any room for the fresh excitement of new love when her body was in turmoil? Every sense was overloaded. Every thought moving at lightning speed. Right now, she was riding an asteroid, blazing through space with little control over where she might end up. What she might crash into.

The drive back to the hospice center was nearly silent. They'd already talked through every scenario and gone round and round on the advantages and disadvantages of going back to be with her grandfather. There wasn't much left to say. Plus, every time Gwen opened her mouth, she thought she might be sick.

Mark's reaction the day before wasn't only going to impact her. Gwen considered calling Leslie, but had decided against it. Gwen didn't have the heart to tell her the fond memories she held of sweet and empathetic Mark hadn't held up. With everything else Leslie had to deal with, Gwen figured it would be more compassionate to leave her fond memories of Mark intact. Leslie deserved that peace.

It took Gwen the elevator ride up to decide she was going to walk into Markus's room. Until that moment she was still ready to run.

This was her paternal grandfather. A person, even a year ago, she never imagined she would meet. Though time with him might be short, it was all the more reason to sit and listen.

Try to cultivate the stories of her heritage before the ones he alone held were gone forever. He'd obviously made his share of mistakes. She wasn't under the illusion that something magical could happen between them. There wouldn't likely be some aha moment of resolution. But anything he told her would be more than she knew now. And she was hungry for that. Famished for a lineage and the building blocks that made her.

"You're back." Renee had the phone pressed to her ear as she stood and waved at Gwen and Griff. There was something painfully sweet about her. A brightness in her eyes that made her look completely unprepared for a letdown. She had the zest of a tiny kitten crossing a busy highway, somehow unaware of the dangers looming all around her.

"We thought we would check in on Markus again," Griff reported as he leaned casually on the nurses' station.

"He's had a good rest this morning, so I am sure he'll be happy for the company." Renee dropped her voice and covered the phone receiver with one hand. She was obviously on hold but still didn't want to overshare with whoever was on the other line. "Did you find his son?"

Gwen shifted nervously from her toes to her heels. "We did. Mark wasn't too excited to see us. He also doesn't want any further communication from anyone here. I don't want to see you get in any trouble. I think it's time to let that go. It's for the best. If he did come here, he'd only cause trouble, and I'm sure that's not going to help either of them. I'm sorry it didn't work out better. I know you were really hoping to bring them together."

Renee gulped and hung up the phone abruptly. Ringing her hands together nervously she looked down the hall to make sure they were still alone. "Apparently this job gets easier. That's what everyone keeps telling me. I love the medical field and helping people. I've always understood there would be losses. Even here, where the statistics for survival are not very favorable, I've managed to be at peace with the outcomes of patients. This is the first time I've watched someone face it alone. Completely alone. He's putting on a brave front, but I can't imagine what it would be like to have no one in the world willing to come visit you on your deathbed. He's not interested in any person of faith coming. He has no friends to speak of. It's haunting me."

"We're here," Griff offered up soothingly. "And you seem to be giving him quite a bit of your time too. He's not alone."

Renee wiped her eyes as the desk phone rang again. "You guys can go in. I've got to catch up on a few things."

Moving toward the room felt different this time. Gwen had no intention of lying. It was pointless to keep the information from him. He was her grandfather and maybe knowing he had some family willing to be with him would matter to him.

"The do-gooders are back," he croaked, adjusting the hose pumping oxygen into his nose. "Now you're going to lay the Bible stuff on me. I'm tethered to this stupid bed. I'm trapped." He pointed to the multiple cords and lines attached to him. She couldn't tell if he kept bringing it up because he hoped they would push a little religion on him.

Gwen slipped her bag off her shoulder and took the seat closest to him. "We're just visiting."

He narrowed his eyes. "For no apparent reason? I still don't buy it. Don't you two have jobs?"

"We do." Griff took a seat and put an arm over the back

of Gwen's chair. His fingers tapped softly on her arm. Just enough to let her know he was there. Ready to hold her up if needed. "Gwen is actually a fancy genetic scientist."

"Do you even know what I do?" She smirked at Griff and watched him scramble for an answer.

"I have a general idea of what you do."

"Stop now while you're ahead, boy," Markus grumbled knowingly.

Her grandfather was sitting within reach and Gwen turned her attention to his face. Studying it now in a way she hadn't yesterday. Looking for the similarities she'd found when she'd met Leslie. Ones she could even spot when she'd briefly seen Mark. As hard as she searched she couldn't see it in Markus. His face was too weathered and drawn from illness to see any of her features there.

"I do have a reason to be here." Gwen sat up a little straighter and cleared her throat. "I'm not sure how to say this." She fidgeted with a loose string at the hem of her shirt, not able to look up at him.

"I'm dying so you may want to come out with it. Don't worry about being indelicate. Lay it on me. If you're here for money or something, I don't have any."

"No." She pursed her lips. "I don't want anything from you. I have everything I need back home. But there is something I have to tell you."

Markus turned to Griff. "Is she always this dramatic?"

"Pretty much. But this time it's warranted." Griff tapped her arm again, obviously trying to encourage her.

Markus looked intrigued. "Well, spit it out. What's this big melodramatic reveal you've got? It had better not be too exciting. I could croak at any moment."

"We lied yesterday when we came to visit and told you we were just random volunteers." Gwen's cheeks blazed hot and red. Admitting they'd lied to him made her feel sick. But it was the only place to start.

"I think I already nailed you for that," Markus said through a cough. "No surprises there."

"I'm your granddaughter." She watched his expression closely, but there was no reaction. He looked completely unaffected by the news as though he hadn't heard it. "Mark is my father."

"Oh." Markus nodded but still didn't react.

"That's all you have to say? Oh?" Gwen sat back, resting heavily on the chair, hoping to feel Griff's hand on her shoulder. He didn't let her down.

"I figured he had some kids. I bet I've got quite a few grandkids. Plus you look so much like Yolanda that I had a suspicion you were part of our family."

"Yolanda?" Gwen turned to Griff, and he shrugged a bit.

"Your grandmother. Mark's mother. You've never seen a picture? I figured he'd have a damn shrine to her. She was a saint. Those kids, especially Mark, worshiped her. You've got her eyes and her hair. Same chin too."

Gwen's hand went to her chin. It was like her grandmother's. Another bit of information she clung desperately to. "I don't know Yolanda, and I don't know Mark." Gwen felt some sense of relief as Markus finally showed some level of surprise.

"You don't know him? What's that mean?"

"I was put up for adoption. He doesn't know I exist. I figured, like you said yesterday, telling you a secret wouldn't hurt."

Markus smirked. "This is quite the turn. Wouldn't it make more sense to tell my son? Shouldn't he know?"

Gwen felt the disappointment creep back in. "I went to his house yesterday. It didn't go so smoothly. I decided I didn't want to tell him. I'm not sure what the point would be if I didn't want him in my life. I'm better off keeping it to myself."

"Really?" Markus looked shocked, his thick brows going up and his mouth turning down.

Griff cut in. "She didn't tell him who she was. She went there to talk to him about you. That's the part that didn't go over well."

"Ah." Markus lit with understanding. "That makes more sense. He hates me. I've given him good reasons to. I bet if you leave me out of the conversation and let him know who you are, it'll go better next time."

Gwen stiffened in the hard plastic chair. "I'm not interested in a next time. Like I said, there would be no point."

"You inherited Yolanda's stubborn streak too. She would never put up with my bull. Called me on it every time. There would have been plenty of times in her life that would have been easier if she would've backed down or given in on something. She never did." His face beamed with pride as he discussed his ex-wife. As though having been married to her somehow made him a better person. "Too bad she had to deal with me. I was not worth it."

"Why? What did you do that was so bad?"

"I think it's all the things I didn't do. I walked out on them when my kids were small. Yolanda had to do it all on her own. She worked a bunch of jobs. Got them all through school."

Gwen still couldn't imagine walking out on family. "You really just left? Why exactly did you go?"

"Why does anyone?" Markus shrugged his bony shoulders. "I was convinced I could do better. Or that I'd be happier with another life. There's a grind with marriage and parenting. Having four kids and living paycheck to paycheck just broke me down."

Markus looked toward the window even though the blinds were pulled shut. "They were better without me. All I ever did was let them down. Gamble away our savings. Show up drunk at some family event. There was no winning with me around. Yolanda did great without me there. It was for the best."

Griff scoffed. "That's convenient."

"Yeah," Markus agreed with a sigh. "I haven't believed it for a while either. You two are young. It's impossible for you to imagine how much regret you can gather up. I've maxed out those emotional credit cards. The best thing I can do is leave this earth quietly. They'll all be better off."

"You don't know that." Gwen felt a pang of pain for his current situation. There was no excusing what he'd done, but did that really mean he had to die without ever making peace?

"I'd say Mark's reaction to you yesterday was pretty clear. He doesn't want to see me and I'm sure his sisters feel the same way." He paused and smiled for the first time. "But you're here. You're family. And I haven't ruined things with you yet."

"Yet? That sounds pretty pessimistic."

"It sounds accurate. Every family member. Every friend. Every job I've had. I blow it. And then I run. It's not a flattering depiction of myself, but at this point"—he motioned to the tubes in his arms—"it's not worth trying to pretend otherwise."

Gwen reached forward and touched his arm. "Well you don't look like you're in running shape at the moment and you're not going to have enough time to ruin things with me."

Markus gave a throaty laugh. "I like dark humor. You two can stay awhile."

"Can you tell me more about my family? Your family? I don't know anything."

"There are only rotten apples on my family tree. You won't be glad to find out about any of them. But don't worry, you grew up far enough away where you won't end up like us. My father is the reason I'm like this. That's not just me trying to lay blame at someone else's feet. He was a hammer, I was his nail. His father was a damn sledgehammer. And his father before that was a jackhammer. Each generation gets a little less destructive, but it's still there. I thought maybe Mark would be different since he wasn't around me. The Ruiz men are toxic and contagious."

Griff shifted his gaze between both of them. "This is depressing. Are you two sure this is how you want to spend this precious time?"

Markus grunted. "You got a better idea? I'm not going to sugarcoat things for the girl."

Griff stood up and walked to the shelf by the window. "Let's play cards. At least then we can have a few laughs."

"Poker?" Markus asked, sitting up a bit.

"We're not betting anything," Griff sighed. "I'd imagine you've honed your card-shark skills?"

"Busted," Markus admitted with a devilish grin. "Are you suggesting Go Fish?"

"No," Gwen cut in, taking the cards from Griff. "Let's play poker. But we don't bet money. We bet stories. Honest stories. Maybe even a few happy ones. I believe you've had a junky life, Markus, but I refuse to believe there haven't been at least a few good times too. You win a hand, you get to ask me something. I win a hand, I ask you. Deal?"

"And what about him?" Markus jutted his chin toward Griff dismissively.

"He's going to go out and get us some authentic Spanish food from whatever place you like best."

"Ah," Markus waggled his finger at her. "You want to get in touch with your Spanish roots? I know just the place."

Griff stood, shooting them both an annoyed look. "Maybe I want to play poker and not be your errand boy."

Gwen looked at Markus and smiled. "Scram, kid, you couldn't hack it with the Ruiz family. We're toxic and contagious."

CHAPTER TWELVE

Mark

Jocelyn looked radiant as she strode up the steps toward his side door. He stepped out early to greet her and drink in the simple elegance of her stride. She was poetry in motion. Her hair was pulled into a ponytail and her oversized cotton shirt hung off one shoulder. Yoga pants clung to her curves. The wine bottle in her hand was one of his favorites, and he looked forward to sharing it with her.

"You didn't have to come out all this way," he said apologetically. "I know the road out here is a little rough."

"It was no trouble at all. I didn't want to cancel our night just because you kicked a wall." She looked down at his foot. It had some gnarly bruises on it and he still believed a couple toes were broken. He decided wrapping it up in an ace bandage would spare her the sight of it.

"I didn't kick the wall, I sort of . . . banged into it." He held the screen door open and she slinked by him, her perfume wafting and enticing him to follow.

"That's how it starts you know. Pretty soon you're going to have to have a traveling nurse here to take care of you."

"You said you were looking for a job," he teased. "I'm sure you could make the outfit look good."

"You wouldn't want me taking care of you. I'm more apt to put you out to pasture like a lame horse." She handed him the wine and he pulled down a couple of his best wineglasses. "Do we need to pad the walls?"

"I was distracted. Pissed, actually."

"What happened?" Jocelyn hopped up to sit on the counter as if she'd been to his house a hundred times.

He liked how comfortable she looked at his place. Handing her a heavily poured glass of wine, he decided to explain.

"My father is in hospice care."

"Oh." Her face crumpled with empathy. "I'm so sorry. I was being insensitive. I didn't realize it was something so serious."

"No." He waived off her apology. "I like that you have a sense of humor. My dad being in hospice care isn't what had me pissed. He and I don't talk. We haven't for decades. He walked out on my mother when I was a kid. He left her to care for four children on her own. It put her in an early grave." He sipped on his wine and thought of his mother. Not only did she work multiple jobs, she usually had perfect attendance. There was no time to get sick. No day where she could pull the covers up over her head and hide in bed. Life moved at a breakneck pace for Yolanda Ruiz and, somehow, she kept up.

"So if it wasn't that, what had you playing soccer with the wall?" She pulled her glass up to her face but didn't sip. Instead she drew in a deep breath and swirled the wine around in her glass.

"There is this nurse at the facility who keeps trying to get in touch with me. She wrote letters and then tracked my number down. I've just been blowing it off. I don't have any interest in seeing him. Well, yesterday another letter shows up. I'm frustrated and I go to throw it out and bam, broken toes."

"She sounds relentless." Finally Jocelyn took a sip of the fragrant red wine. She closed her eyes and hummed, looking impressed by the rich flavor.

"It gets worse. Right then, she and some guy show up here. They literally tracked me down and showed up at my door. My foot was throbbing. I was really frustrated. I acted like a complete ass to them. I kicked them off my property, and I'm pretty sure I threatened litigation if they came back."

"Ouch." She cringed and he knew he deserved that reaction. "That was a bad day."

"Not my proudest moment. It's been eating me up, actually. It's not this girl's fault that my dad got into her head. Who knows what he's convinced her of by this point? He's a master manipulator. That's actually too generous. He's a con artist at best."

"And yet you're so well adjusted." Her words were somewhere between playfully teasing and challenging him to go on. To open up more.

He raised a finger in her direction, putting her on notice that he knew what she was doing. "Don't try to goad me into baring my soul here. I know your tricks now. I still can't believe I told you I don't like being retired. I had no intention of publicizing that."

"You didn't put up much of a fight. You folded like a cheap suit. I'm going to have to start charging you for therapy sessions soon."

"I'll pay you in dinners. And the second bottle of wine we drink tonight." He gestured toward the large wine rack in the corner of the room.

"Two bottles. You expect me to be able to navigate that winding road around the lake to get back home?" She cocked a brow and smiled behind her wineglass.

"I'm happy to take the couch tonight."

"A platonic sleepover? Just a couple of girlfriends sipping on wine and falling asleep on the couch." She scoffed. "You must think I'm a fool."

"I think you're lovely."

"What if I piss you off and you kick me off your property like those two young kids yesterday?" She could barely get the words out through her laughter.

Mark stepped back and threw a hand over his heart as though she'd just shot an arrow through it. "You are ruthless. I feel terrible. It's killing me."

"You know how to get in touch with the girl. She's sent you all those letters. Call and apologize tomorrow."

"Therapy and free advice? How lucky am I?"

"No one said it's free. Now come elevate your bad foot and watch terrible reality television with me. That is what we do when we're feeling bad. If you're going to be one of my girlfriends, you'll have to play the part." She hopped down gracefully off her perch on the counter and led him toward the couch.

As they sat down on the couch he couldn't help but ask the burning question. "You don't think I'm a complete monster for not wanting to see my father before he dies? Isn't that the humane thing to do?"

"Honestly?" She hesitated, forcing him to answer.

"What's the point otherwise?"

"If it were me, I'd go see him. No matter what happened or who he was, I'd make time to go see him. Even if it didn't change how I felt about him."

"But why? I already know everything I need to about him. I have nothing I feel compelled to say. I wouldn't forgive him for what he did to my mother. So why go?"

"Because if you don't, that's the person you are. It has nothing to do with the person he is. You're the guy who held a grudge. Just because you feel a certain way now doesn't mean you'll feel that way in ten or twenty years. Think about all your views and opinions when you were in your twenties. I think you've evolved."

"I'd hope so. I was pretty sure I'd end up being in a rock band. There was a mullet involved."

"Sometime down the road, maybe even when you're in the same position as him, you'll think about how you handled this. You'll think about whether or not you went to see him. It might matter then." Her face fell serious and she put her glass of wine down on the coffee table. "My mother passed away in a car accident. I was out of town and I didn't make it back in time to say goodbye before they had to let her go. I've often wondered if it was better or worse to go quick. A long illness gives perspective and time that a sudden death doesn't. I'd imagine it's more complicated than that, but I do think about it from time to time."

"I'm sorry about your mother. I'm guessing your relationship with her was a little better than the one I have with my father."

She put her hands up disarmingly. "You asked my opinion. But it's your choice to make. My only suggestion is that you make that choice with your ghost of Christmas future. Old man Mark, many many years from now, might have feelings about this. But it'll be too late to do anything about it."

"I appreciate all those manys."

Jocelyn pulled her legs up onto the couch and curled them in. Her socks were comically fuzzy. There was a silliness to her that he appreciated.

"Can I ask you another question?" She practically purred out the words, obviously trying not to scare him off with her prying. But he didn't mind her interest in who he was. The fact that she'd come into this, whatever it was, without the idea that they'd turn into some serious relationship made him feel at ease. Mostly because, unlike some women, he could tell she meant it when she said she wasn't interested in anything serious.

"I'm an open book. Ask away."

"Is your dad the reason you decided not to have kids? I know we've both had our share of people judging us about our choices regarding parenting. So don't answer if you don't want to. I've just known people who grew up with crap parents and decided they didn't want to take a chance at doing the same thing."

Mark hadn't even been close at guessing what her question would be. The shock likely showed on his face. He leaned back on the couch and rested an arm over the back of the plush cushions. "That's a good question."

"One you don't have to answer," she reminded him.

"No, I don't mind." He thought through the answer for a moment. "I've never really felt like father material. My dad certainly made me realize that a child deserves more than some half-assed effort and then desertion. But he wasn't what made me definitively decide marriage and kids weren't right for me. There was a point in time when I actually saw myself settling down."

"Whoa, she must have been quite the woman."

"She was," Mark admitted, the memories he'd buried flooding back in. "We met at work. She had a couple of young kids and her husband had left her. It was just a fling. Or that's how it started. On paper it didn't make any sense. My career was taking off. She was trying to hold her life together. But from the first moment I saw her I just couldn't take my eyes off her. Then the kids got me."

"Got you?"

"They were so sweet and I really took to them right out of the gate. Leslie needed help. She was spread too thin. Her husband had walked out the same way my father had. But in spite of all that, she had this great sense of humor. And the way she worked so hard for her kids. I was just in awe of her." Mark conjured up the memory of Leslie's face. And then ached at the thought of their last goodbye. It was so anticlimactic. Unfinished.

"And that made you not want to have children?"

"I was all in, actually. For the first time in my life I could see myself committing to someone and not hesitating. The kids had these great little personalities. Her youngest was just a baby but he'd smile up at me and, damn it, would just melt my heart. Then we both had to move on from the project we were working on. She was based on the East Coast. My next project brought me back here."

"You called it off?"

"No," Mark said, the old ache coming back to his chest. "I was actually going to try to make it work. Things kind of blew up at work and then I had personal stuff going on."

"What happened?"

"My mother got sick. Pneumonia. She ended up pulling through, but for another couple of weeks it took over my life. Leslie and I needed to take a break anyway. Some other things had to blow over. I thought it wouldn't matter. Nothing would change the way things were between us."

"It sounds like it did change."

"I bought a ring," Mark admitted, feeling his cheeks flush. "I was going to fly there and propose. The day before I bought my ticket she called me. She was talking to her husband again. She thought they might work it out. The reason she was calling was to tell me how grateful she was for my help when she needed it the most. She cried. I wanted to talk her out of going back to that deadbeat. I wanted to tell her she deserved so much better, and I could be the one to give it to her and the boys. Instead, I looked down at the ring in my hand and wished her luck."

"What a heartbreak." Jocelyn sighed, covering her own heart with her delicate hand. "You must have fallen to pieces."

"I realized very quickly what it felt like to get wrecked by someone. And it felt a lot like karma. In my younger days I hadn't done as good of a job explaining to women what my priorities were. I'd strung some people along. I'd broken hearts. And that day was the first time I understood how bad it could hurt. From that point on I decided there was no way I was going to put anyone through that again. Any kind of relationship I get into is full disclosure right out of the gate. No confusion, no miscommunication. Realizing I wouldn't see those boys again, knowing Leslie hadn't felt the same way about me that I did about her, was eye-opening. I had to readjust my outlook."

"I readjusted my outlook when I picked the soon-to-be ex-husband. I'm starting to worry that's just a pretty way to say *settling*." Her wine was back in her hand and she swirled it around a bit more.

"Maybe you're right, but I haven't done much looking back over the years. My career was always full. Lots of friends. Great vacations. And fine women to keep me company. All of that with none of the heartbreak."

"Yeah. I'm in the heartbreak zone."

"You're handling it well."

"I'm compartmentalizing. When I get back home and it's quiet, I don't look nearly as optimistic."

He reached out and touched her arm gingerly. "Then don't go sit at home." Their eyes locked and he watched her lashes flutter with excitement. Leaning over he grabbed the remote and waved it victoriously at her. "We're going to watch baseball. No reality television marathons."

"Put baseball on and the reality television show tantrum is going to happen right here in real life."

"That sounds exciting." He pointed the remote at the television and dared her to stop him. "Go easy on the furniture. Some of it's one of a kind."

It had been too long since he'd had this kind of fun. Letting his guard down with Jocelyn felt effortless. Mark had been so focused on the negative things that came with retirement, he'd overlooked how free he felt. There was no persona to uphold. No need to worry about who was angling for his job or what downturn the economy might take. He could simply feel whatever he wanted and talk openly about it. What a strange idea.

"Have you given these shows a chance?" Jocelyn put her wineglass down and climbed over to his side of the couch. She plucked the remote from his hands, and he couldn't even pretend to put up a fight. "You're retired now; you should understand how the wives of famous basketball players deal with their interpersonal problems. Or how a family of twenty or so kids handles homeschool."

"Twenty kids?" Mark cocked a brow up and folded his arms over his chest. "People watch this?"

"No," she said, shaking her head dramatically. "People binge-watch this."

CHAPTER THIRTEEN

Mark

Mark walked down to the pier with his hands tucked into his pockets. It was laughable how his opinion of the lake had changed, literally overnight. It was the way Jocelyn sat on the back porch. The air was still cool and her mug of coffee had streams of steam billowing up from it. She was curled in a chair while ribbons of light from the rising sun warmed her face. With an unwavering focus she continued to stare out at every detail. He watched her as she looked on at the scenery and somehow the value of it all increased. The way she described it, all the trees really were dancing. The ripples on the lake did look like art. The hills in the distance would be a great place to hike. She was right.

It was basic psychology, maybe. Someone else picked up and enjoyed the toy he'd discarded and now suddenly it was something special again. Jocelyn stood and stretched like a cat as she leaned against the railing. When she had asked about the pier earlier, it was as if he were noticing it for the first time.

Before she left, they made plans to have a picnic on the pier sometime soon. So he thought he'd better go check it out. He'd walked on it when he'd first decided to buy the house but hadn't been down since.

Stepping onto the planks he moved slowly and tentatively, shifting his weight to look for weak spots. It felt sturdier than it looked. His sore foot ached a bit but the two pain relievers he'd popped this morning were helping. It hadn't dulled his hangover headache completely, but he was getting by. They'd managed to drink two bottles of wine while watching a ridiculous dance competition followed by a reality dating show. The lineup never ended, and while the shows seemed batty, he was glad when another would start. Every time he dramatically argued why the shows were nonsense, she'd take up the other side of the debate. Hour after hour, late into the night, they'd bickered and joked.

As he reached the end of the pier he drew in a deep, centering breath. Compelled by a whim, he shook off his shoes and tugged off his socks. The cool water would be good for his injured foot. He got to the end of the dock and dunked his feet in. That was something a child would do, but nothing he'd done as a child. There were never any vacations by a lake. No vacations at all that he could remember. Closing his eyes he imagined his mother sitting there at the edge of the pier, watching over her children. They'd be splashing and dunking each other. Soaking in the fleeting daylight. Dinner would be simmering on the stove. Marshmallows ready to be roasted for dessert. He and his sisters could have felt like children. They'd have had a brief shot at being carefree and unburdened by the worry of poverty.

It wasn't realistic to imagine that, if his father had stayed, there would have been any family vacations to reminisce about. The man had gambled away the family savings at least twice that Mark knew of. Surely the family would have been in worse shape if he'd stayed around.

Opening his eyes he thought of what a crass man his father could be. And with a pit in his stomach, he remembered how rude he'd been a couple of days ago to those kids who came to talk to him. The one measure that always mattered to Mark was that he was not like his father.

Reaching for his cell phone he decided the biggest thing that always separated him from the failures of his father was his ability to make it right. Calling the number, he hoped it went to voice mail. He could still make it right without having to talk to anyone. Unfortunately Renee picked up.

"Hello?"

"Hi, Renee, this is Mark Ruiz."

"Oh, hello." He heard rustling papers and she sounded like she was shifting uneasily. "I didn't expect you to call."

"I owe you an apology for the way I acted the other day. I was surprised by your visit, and I'll admit the subject of my father makes me quite tense. But that's no excuse for how I talked to you." He moved his feet in a circular motion, disturbing the surface of the lake.

"That wasn't me," Renee said in a tiny voice.

"Don't worry. I'm not going to call my lawyer. I wouldn't get you in any kind of trouble. I just wanted to call to apologize."

"No really, it wasn't me. Griff and Gwen came out to see you. I promise, it wasn't me."

He remembered the man saying his name was Griff. "Oh, well could you pass my apology on to them then? I just didn't want to leave it unsaid. Whichever of your coworkers came here, tell them I'm sorry."

"They don't work here. Gwen is Markus's granddaughter."

"What?"

"Yes, I didn't know it at first but she came back the next day and told me that she's Markus's granddaughter."

"She said that the day after she left my property?"

"Yes."

"I see." Mark was putting the pieces together. This couple came out, saw his sports car and the private lakefront home and realized maybe Markus Senior had more than he was letting on. This couple was no better than his father. He chuckled at the crappy luck.

"I think I know all my nieces and nephews. She is no relative of my father or mine. I suppose he could have some illegitimate children scattered around and they could have had children, but I doubt that's the case. You've got yourself a couple of con artists trying to scam a con artist. It's karma."

"Um"—Renee drew in a deep breath—"I don't think I should really get too much more involved. I've really done too much already, and I'm sorry for how I acted. I had just wanted Markus to have the opportunity to connect with some family and have some peace before he passed. It seems like Gwen is going to keep visiting for now."

"That will certainly help her try to make a play for

anything of his. She should know he probably doesn't have anything. It's a waste of time."

"Mr. Ruiz," Renee said meekly, "she's a lovely girl and they seem to be getting on very well. I know I crossed the line with you. I had no right to send those letters or try to call you. I haven't been in my job very long, and I let my emotions get the better of me."

"I understand," Mark lied. He didn't know what it was like to work in a building where the majority of people passed away rather than got better and went home. It was likely a heavy toll. He could understand how Renee may have thought she was helping. "Just watch yourself around this Gwen girl. I doubt she's really any kind of relative of his. She certainly isn't one of mine. Keep an eye on your purse when she's around. I've learned an opportunistic thief is the worst kind."

"While I have you on the line, was there anything else you wanted to know about your father?"

"No," he replied flatly. "He's a stranger to me."

Renee hummed. "All right. Well, have a good day."

"You too."

Mark tucked his phone back in his pocket and his shoulders slumped. This call was meant to clear his conscience and make him feel better. He was feeling worse now. Renee had planted a seed. No, it was a ticking time bomb in his brain. Of course he'd want to know more about Gwen now. Was there any risk to himself or his sisters with this girl trying to ingratiate herself to his dying father? He'd now need to reach out to his sisters and give them a heads-up about her. It would be up to them to decide if they wanted to see their father, but they should at least know about Gwen. Like him, they wouldn't be surprised that some other grifter had turned up, looking to take advantage.

A large bird swooped down from a tree and dunked into the lake, searching for a snack. Mark lay back and tucked his arms beneath his head as he stared up at the expansive cloudless sky. He should go down to that facility and see what was going on for himself. He should see this supposed granddaughter and toss her out of there. What kind of person would prey on a dying old man? He could go there without having to see his father. Rattle these two kids enough for them to hightail it out and go find some other person to try to swindle.

Now he had another reason to put his watch on tomorrow. An appointment with some lowlife crooks.

CHAPTER FOURTEEN

Gwen

By her fourth visit Gwen was feeling comfortable in Markus's room. Adding some flowers to the windowsill was her best attempt at brightening up the place. She'd also dropped the formalities of asking him if he wanted company and instead just grabbed her chair and the deck of cards as she slid the table over his bed.

"Ready to lose again?" Gwen asked with a wry smile as she shuffled. Today Griff had opted to explore the town, which she knew was his way of giving them space. He planned to come for the second half of the visit around lunchtime. If it made Markus more apt to speak freely with just her there, Griff wanted to make sure that would happen.

"No cards today," Markus croaked out. His eyes fluttered, but didn't open all the way.

"Oh, come on, you can sleep when you're dead." This

type of joke was exactly what made Markus laugh the hardest. The darker and more morbid it was, the longer he'd enjoy it. But this time he didn't laugh. Instead there was just a long moan and a weak attempt at waving his hand.

"Are you all right?" she asked, putting the cards down and moving in closer to him. "Do you want me to get the nurse?" Renee was off duty this morning, but Gwen had greeted the other nurse just a moment before. She could hustle back to the desk and have her come in.

Markus only shook his head. With the slightest flick of his calloused finger he pointed to the seat by the bed. He just wanted her to sit. To stay.

There had been these tiny parts of Gwen that held out hope. Maybe he'd have more good days than bad. Maybe, even though the doctors all agreed he wouldn't, there was a chance he'd get better. The reality was much more likely going to be more days like today. Until they ran out of days.

"Hippo," he whispered, his eyes still closed. "Can you take care of Hippo?"

"Your fish?" she asked, leaning in close. "I think Andrea is taking care of him. She may not want to part with him. You might have to put it in your will."

This time Markus chuckled a little.

"Gwen," the nurse called from the doorway. "Could you come out here for a moment?"

Gwen patted Markus's hand gently. "I'll be right back." She braced herself for bad news. It wasn't surprising news. Markus had a very clear-cut prognosis. But still, she assumed the nurse was about to give her something more final and concrete. Her stomach sank.

When she rounded the corner of the room she saw Mark.

Her father was standing there, stone-faced and angry as he had been when they'd met him at his side door. But he was here. That had to be a good sign.

Her face flushed as she tried to find the right words.

His voice was direct and unfriendly. "You look like the cat who swallowed the canary. Didn't think I'd get wise to you?"

"Uh, excuse me?" Gwen tried to process his question.

"You need to leave here before I call the police. I may not have a relationship with my father, but I'll be damned if you're going to come in while he's on his deathbed. I may not want anything from him but my sisters or their kids might."

Gwen looked toward the nurse but she shuffled away with a look of shock on her face.

"Mark, I'm not trying to take anything from him." She raised her hands disarmingly to show they were empty. "I'm visiting with him. He's dying."

"I know he's dying. I also know that I just heard you ask him about putting you in his will. The nurse said he's barely conscious today. What a great day to close on the details. You should know, though, I've kept a close enough watch on his life to tell you there isn't much of his to go around. You picked a bad target."

"He's not my target," Gwen fired back, hot angry tears in her eyes. "I was talking about his fish. He asked me to take care of it for him and I told him Andrea, his old neighbor, had Hippo now. If he wanted me to take care of the fish, Andrea might not give it up. We were joking." She wiped at her eyes and leaned against the wall. The accusations were harsh enough, but Gwen found it most difficult to believe this man was her father. The man before her, with his angry glare, was half her DNA.

"Hippo?"

"That's the name of the fish." Gwen gulped. "And if you would listen to me for a minute I could explain why I'm here."

"I'm not going to listen to you." He folded his hands across his chest and continued to stare down at her. "Renee already told me the story you're spinning about being his granddaughter. I don't think so."

Gwen let out a wild laugh. She couldn't believe where this moment had brought them both. "Mark"—she propped her hands on her hips—"he is my grandfather. I'm sure of it. Because I look like Yolanda, don't I?"

"My mother," he said, rolling his eyes. "You've convinced him you look like my mother?"

She didn't speak. She only stood there, letting him take in her features. If the veil of anger started to melt away maybe he would see it for himself. "Well, there is a slight resemblance, but you could have just as easily gotten lucky. Maybe you're good and did some research for the right family first. I know my sisters. They didn't have any children and not tell me about them. Now I'm going to ask you again to leave." He pointed at the elevator but she was not going to move. She'd made up her mind. If Mark was going to back her into the corner, she was going to use the truth to punch her way out.

"Yolanda is my grandmother, Markus is my grandfather. On my paternal side." She watched his face twist up quizzically.

"Ah, no. They had one son. Me. I don't have any children."

"My mother is Leslie Laudon. I'm twenty-six years old." She felt the urge to step back, as if she'd just set a timer on a bomb and it could blow any second.

"Leslie?" That had been a trigger. Enough to make him take a stumbling step back. "She had two boys."

"Yes, and then she had me. Twenty-six years ago. Remember what you were doing then? How are your math skills?" Gwen tried not to sound too arrogant, but Mark had come in hot, and it was time to make sure he heard her.

His hand moved across his forehead as though he were trying to process the information. "No. That's not right. Leslie and I weren't together very long."

"So maybe it's your biology skills that need some work. It doesn't take very long to make a child."

"There is no way." Mark took two steps back as though Gwen's insane thinking might be contagious. "Leslie never told me anything. She would have said something to me. She went back to her husband."

"I only just found her," Gwen said somberly. "I don't know her any better than you do. You'd have to ask her why she never told you."

"Found her?" Mark's brows crashed downward.

"She put me up for adoption." This wasn't how she had wanted to have this conversation. It was expected that Mark would be stunned, and Gwen felt a great responsibility to deliver the news tenderly. Gwen, when she originally considered meeting him, anticipated answering his questions and gradually unfurling the story. Instead this was more like a deluge of punches, each one hitting him with a shock, back to back, with no time to steady himself.

"She what?" His voice was sharp and loud. When a

patient shuffled tentatively by them, he quieted some. "She put you up for adoption?"

"Maybe we should go somewhere to talk. You must have a lot of questions. I'm not sure I'll be able to answer them all. Leslie has just begun to share things with me. But maybe if we could have a cup of coffee somewhere it would help."

"Gwen?" Markus called from his bed. His raspy voice echoed into the hallway. "Are you still here?"

"You should go sit with him." Mark's face was pale, his mouth slack as he searched for something more to say.

"So should you." She gestured for him to come. "Please, I know this is a lot of information, but I don't want you to leave like this."

"I have to go." Mark turned on his heel and strode away quickly. She couldn't blame him. Running was all she wanted to do some days.

"Who was that?" Markus asked, shifting himself up as best he could on the pillow.

"It was no one," she said, not wanting to give him false hope that his son might be coming back.

"You fighting with that boyfriend of yours? What's his name? Grape?"

"You know his name is Griff, and you know he's not my boyfriend." She sank into the chair and tried to pretend her heart wasn't thudding against her ribs.

"Right, you two are just friends. I've seen enough people in my day to know when it's more than that. So trouble in paradise?"

"Men are stubborn," she said, grabbing the cards again and shuffling them. "Are you awake enough now for me to beat you in cards?"

"I'm a good listener," Markus said with a weak smile. "Deal and tell me what the problem is."

"I don't want to talk about it. Tell me more about Mark. What was he like when he was a kid?"

"Mark?" He took the cards she dealt him and looked closely at them. "He was a very serious child. I guess maybe he had to be to make up for me. I always knew he'd be successful. He did well in school. Picked up odd jobs around the neighborhood when he could. I think he had the most successful paper route in town."

"What did he like to do?"

"Like hobbies?" Markus furrowed his brows and looked as though he were trying to remember. "He loved the movies. It wasn't often he'd have the money to go see one. But he'd sweep up the lobby and clean the popcorn stand at the end of the night in exchange for a chance to go see a movie. That kid knew how to hustle. He could barter his way into anything. He wouldn't admit it but he's a lot like me, he just used his powers for good."

"When is the last time you talked to him?"

"Years." Markus shook his head and corrected himself. "Decades. He was probably only a little older than you. He'd gotten a job at this small law office. He was mostly doing paperwork. Running to the court, I think. I got arrested for writing some bad checks. I went into the office he worked at. I thought maybe he could talk to one of the lawyers there and get me a deal."

"That didn't go over well?"

"He made it very clear I was never to contact him again. He said if I did, he'd use all his favors to make sure I went away for my crimes for the maximum time. That was as angry as I've ever seen him. All the stuff I did and he never looked at me the way he did that day."

"After that you just left him alone?" Gwen knew people who had fractured relationships. But in her experience, with time they found a way back to each other, even if things didn't go back to the way they were before. To go all these years without a single word seemed extreme. She'd heard Markus tell dreadful stories of how he'd hurt his family. How he'd let them down and lost his right to be their father. Still no matter how she tried to put herself in Mark's shoes, she couldn't imagine a scenario where she wouldn't have walked in there right then. How could he have gotten that close? All the way to his father's hospital room door, and not come in?

"After that day I knew he was really done with me. It was written all over his face. A couple of my daughters kept in touch here and there and I would ask about Mark. But he had told them not to tell me anything about him. The man can hold a grudge."

Gwen worried if that would carry over to her as well. Would Mark resent being ambushed with the news and hold that against her? If that was the kind of man she was dealing with, maybe it was better to let it all go.

"Hey," Griff said in a cheery voice as he knocked lightly on the door. "I brought those sandwiches you said were the best in town." He held up a grease-covered brown paper bag.

"Your peace offering?" Markus asked, an angry edge to his voice. "Are we forgiving him?"

"We are," Gwen said, making a face at Griff, expecting him to play along. "All is forgiven. Especially since he comes bearing gifts." She hurried to him and took the sandwiches. "Do you feel like eating, Markus?"

"You know, you can call me something else," Markus said, clearing his throat nervously.

"Mr. Ruiz?" Gwen asked with a smirk.

"I have grandkids. I've just never met them. No one has ever called me anything like Grandpa."

"You want me to call you Grandpa?" Gwen asked, the smile melting away from her face.

"No," Markus barked. "I said if you wanted to you could. I don't care what you call me."

"Careful," Griff cut in. "She's got a knack for calling people names. She swears like a sailor. You might regret it."

"I do not," Gwen argued. "But I don't think I'll call you Grandpa. You don't seem like a grandpa to me."

"Fine." Markus put his cards down and waved for his sandwich. "I don't care."

"What did you call your grandparents?"

"Ha." Markus let out a hearty laugh as he unwrapped his sandwich. "Well, my grandparents only spoke Spanish. We called him *abuelo* or *abuelito*. I couldn't say either when I was a kid so it turned into Lito."

"Lito," Gwen said, nodding at the idea. "That suits you."

Markus nibbled a little on the edge of the sandwich and shrugged. "Yeah, that's fine with me. You two staying for lunch?" He gestured toward their chairs, pretending to be a bit annoyed.

"Yeah, Lito." Gwen smiled and looped her arm in Griff's.

Griff sat and balanced his sandwich in his lap. There was only room on the little table for Gwen and Markus to put their food. "Can I call you Lito too?" Griff knew exactly what Markus would think of that.

"You can call me Mr. Ruiz."

CHAPTER FIFTEEN

Gwen

It was the first time she'd insisted on being alone. She wasn't hungry. She didn't want to talk about it. Griff tried to be supportive, but all she wanted was some solace. Her father, the man she'd wondered about most of her life, had just yelled at her and stormed off. He had no way to get in touch with her even if he wanted to. And she wouldn't dare call the number she'd found for him.

The strong Long Island iced tea she'd ordered wasn't very appealing. As she swirled the tiny straw around, she watched the ice dancing. In a couple days, she'd need to go home. Everything was up to Mark now. If he wanted to know more, he'd need to find her. He'd need to make the next move. And she was certain he wouldn't.

When her phone rang with an unfamiliar number, hope ballooned up, nearly popping as she juggled her phone to her ear. The hotel lobby was quiet so she kept her voice low as she answered.

"Hey, Gwen," a familiar voice said, and she shot up straight.

"Ryan?" There was a little inflection in the way he said her name that was so unmistakably him.

"Yeah, how are you?" His voice was unnaturally chipper.

"Um, I'm good, how are you?"

"I know, this is out of the blue. I'm sorry. I called your mom yesterday." He drew in a deep breath. "I felt terrible about not calling for your graduation."

"It's no problem. I know you're busy." The petty part of her wanted to mention his girlfriend, but she bit her tongue.

"I shouldn't be too busy to congratulate you on something you've been working on for so long. I'm really proud of you. I hate what you and I turned into. I never thought there would come a time in my life where I couldn't call you and tell you what was going on with me." Ryan's words ran together the way they did when he got nervous. It was odd to think of him as worried now. Right out of the gate in their relationship they'd been comfortable with each other. Both committed to honesty. Until suddenly, at the end, Gwen had failed in that department.

"Thank you," Gwen said, still feeling awkward about the conversation. Keeping the truth from Ryan about her miscarriage was something that kept her up at night. Staring up at the ceiling of her bedroom she'd imagine what her life would've been like if she'd leaned into him instead of leaning away. "It's nice to be finished with school."

"Your mother also told me you were in California. What part?" His voice rose a bit with a hopefulness she couldn't place. Why would he care if she were in the same state as him?

"I'm just outside LA right now."

"Really? You aren't too far from me then. Rumor has it you found your birth mother. The whole neighborhood back home has been gossiping about it." He chuckled, presumably at the idea of the rumor mill they both used to despise. "I had no idea that was even something you were considering. How did I not know that?" There was a pain in his voice as though there was a party he hadn't been invited to.

"It wasn't something I considered until last year. Then it was all I considered. To the point I ended up in the hospital."

"Gwen are you serious?" Ryan's concern was genuine. "I had no idea. I feel awful I didn't try to call you sooner. I just wasn't sure what you wanted. I was trying to give you some space. But maybe I should have done more to let you know I was there if you needed me."

"I knew that, Ryan. I knew if I called you, you'd be there for me. It wasn't you, it was me."

He scoffed, snorting out a laugh. "That's a tough phrase for me right now. Mandy said the same thing to me a couple weeks ago. I'm starting to get a complex. One minute my relationships seem solid and the next I'm being consoled with the oldest breakup line in the book. I don't get it. I try to be a good boyfriend."

"You were an amazing boyfriend," Gwen asserted, nearly knocking over her drink. "I'm sorry you two broke up. I'm sure it wasn't anything you did."

"Were you cheating?" Ryan asked bluntly. "I'm not trying to be crude. Mandy was cheating. I had no idea. I was completely blindsided."

She finally recognized the odd tone in his voice. He'd been drinking, and he had a good buzz. "Ryan, that's really terrible. I can't imagine how bad that sucks right now. But no, that's not what it was for us."

"It's just—" Ryan cleared his throat, trying to gain some control of his thoughts. "If it's me, I want to know what it is. Because I feel like I'm doing it right. I treated you well, didn't I? With Mandy I was working a lot. That's what she said. I was never around for her."

"That's not a reason to cheat," Gwen comforted. "You were always very supportive. I felt very loved, and I loved you very much."

"Until, very suddenly, you didn't anymore. I think that's my question, Gwen. What changed? I was going to marry you. We were going to move out here together. What happened? I have to know, because I can't go through this again. I can't be completely in love with someone only to feel like at any moment they're going to walk out."

Gwen felt the weight of her lies pressing down on her. "Ryan, honestly, it wasn't anything you did or didn't do."

"Was there someone else?" His voice was pleading and desperate. "You can tell me. Look how much time has passed. We were always upfront with each other."

"We were." Her throat stung as she tried to hold back her lie. "I'm so sorry. I want to explain. I really do. But I don't want to tell you over the phone."

"I'll come to you."

She heard him shuffling around. "Ryan, no. I'll come to you. Just send me an address. A coffee shop or something. I can meet you."

He groaned. "I made this all about me. I'm being a selfish

idiot. I'm so sorry. You're here for your father, right? Your mom told me that. Maybe I can make some calls and help you find him. I work with a security firm. They can find anyone." He sounded frantic now. She'd never heard him like this in the years they were together.

"Ryan, it's fine. I already found him. Just tell me where to find you. I'll be there."

"Gwen, I'm not doing that great." His voice was gravelly.

"I know. I'll come see you. It'll be all right. Text me an address."

She placed her phone on the bar and pushed her drink away. She wouldn't be finishing it now.

"Going to waste that perfectly good drink?" Griff asked, sliding onto the stool next to her. "You all right?"

Wiping the tears from her cheeks, she turned on her stool toward him and grabbed his face. "You trust me?"

His cheeks were squished beneath her grip, and he gave a comical nod of agreement.

"Ryan just called. He's drunk and very upset. I want to go see him. I think I need to tell him the truth. But you need to know it's not anything more than that." She let his cheeks go and waited for him to say something. Griff was a reasonable guy. Always one to offer some kind of levity in these moments. But she knew instantly by the look on his face that wasn't going to happen this time.

"What's he upset about?" He leaned back and slid her drink toward him, taking a sip.

"His girlfriend broke up with him. She was cheating." Gwen's cheek's felt hot. If the roles were reversed and Griff's former girlfriend wanted to see him, she'd certainly have some questions. Her phone chirped with a text message. It was the address from Ryan. "Say something."

"There isn't too much for me to say. You know I'm never going to be the guy who tells you what you can and can't do."

"If you don't want me to go—"

He shook his head. "Please don't finish that sentence. You can make your own choices. If you want to go see your very upset ex-boyfriend and console him after his breakup, that's a choice you have to make."

"That's not a fair characterization. I've been keeping something from Ryan. I think I should tell him about the miscarriage. The way we ended things was unfair."

"Is he drunk?" Griff raised a challenging brow.

She considered lying, but Griff deserved more than that. "He's had some drinks, I think. But that doesn't change anything. I'm not looking to have anything with Ryan. That part of my life is over. You're the only thing I want."

Griff reached a hand up and touched her cheek. "I love you. It scares the hell out of me how much I love you." He leaned in and kissed her. There was no hesitation. No, moment of wondering if they were making the right choice. This was the kiss she'd been waiting on for as long as she could remember.

He slid off his stool and pulled her in close to him as his lips parted hers. Every single ache, worry, and anxiety left her body. It was only his lips, his swirling tongue, and his hands clutched firmly on her hips. When he pulled back his eyes were searching her face, begging for some kind of reaction.

"I love you too," she whispered, pressing her lips to his again. "I'm tired of waiting for the right moment." She looped her arms around his neck. "I know we're supposed to be logical about all of this. I know I'm a mess right now. But I want to be that mess with you."

"Nothing is different today than yesterday. All the reasons we said we would wait are still there." He ran his thumb over his cheek. "I just don't care anymore."

"Me either."

"Come upstairs. Let's forget everything. It'll all be waiting for us tomorrow. But let's not let it ruin tonight." He pulled her against him and waggled his brows at her.

"Griff," Gwen moaned, dropping her gaze toward the ground. "I told him I would come see him. I've held on to this too long. The way I left things, it wasn't fair."

Griff deflated against her, his grip loosening. "Gwen, it's late. Your secret will still be there tomorrow. At least he'll be sober when he hears it."

She dropped her forehead to his shoulder. "I have to do this first. Before you and I—"

He pulled the keys from his pocket and handed them to her. "Be careful." Griff stepped out of her way. He could have told her to drive careful. But that wasn't what he meant. Or not entirely. It was a warning to be careful with his heart. With her choices. With their future.

"I will," she promised. "I won't be long."

CHAPTER SIXTEEN

Gwen

It wasn't a coffee shop. It wasn't a diner. The address he'd given her was an apartment building. Presumably his.

Damn.

Ryan was waiting out on the stoop, his hands stuffed into his pockets. His button-down shirt was wrinkled as though he'd untucked it from his khakis. The last time she'd seen him, his hair was short. Now it was grown out and styled heavily with gel, though locks were out of place.

He moved toward the car with a nervous energy that didn't suit him. Ryan was a nerd. She didn't mean it as an insult. He was a self-proclaimed geek, and she had loved him for it. He studied hard and it'd paid off. He loved all things sci-fi. But he owned those things about himself. There was a cool energy about him. Now, as she rounded the front of the car she noticed how tense he looked.

"Thanks for coming. Was it a long ride?" He pulled her in for a tight hug. It was the strangest sensation to be in his arms again. Their last hug had been a tear-filled goodbye, one of his boxes in his free arm as he embraced her with the other. This was different. He wrapped himself around her like they'd done on their best days.

"It was about twenty minutes," she said, pulling out of his arms. "I thought we'd grab a cup of coffee."

"I made a pot. I've already had a cup. I obviously needed to get a little sober. I'm sorry I was such a mess when I called. I didn't want to put all that on you."

"You weren't wrong, we do need to talk."

"Come up." He gestured with his head toward the front steps of his apartment building.

"I can't stay too long," she cautioned. "Just one cup."

He smelled the same. She didn't know what she expected. Maybe that his new girlfriend had changed the laundry detergent. Or had bought him some new cologne. But apparently not. The apartment was another moment of pause for her. He gave her the tour, and it was eerie how many of his things had memories tied to them.

"You kept pictures of us?" Gwen asked, looking at the photograph of them on one of their ski trips. "I can't imagine that went over too well."

"Mandy always knew you were something special to me. She wasn't over here that much anyway, so it wasn't really an issue."

"She didn't live here?" Gwen had just assumed by their social media pictures and updates that their relationship was pretty serious.

"She was not a believer in traditional relationship structures. "Living together felt"—he made air quotes and rolled his eyes—"*claustrophobic*." There were some red flags. I'm ready to admit that now."

"You were great to live with. She didn't know what she was missing. You were way better at laundry than I was. Oh, and that chicken marsala recipe you used to make was to die for."

He poured her a cup of coffee just the way she liked it, in her favorite old mug. "I didn't realize I kept this mug. You can take it with you. I know you always liked it."

"My mom probably spilled all sorts of news to you, right? You know they gave me the house? I'm moving there and working at a lab in Connecticut now."

"I'm not going to get Millie in trouble," Ryan said sweetly as they took a seat on the couch. "She may have mentioned a couple things. She did tell me you were out here looking for your biological father. You found him?"

"I did."

"How's that going? People back home seemed to think finding your biological mother was a positive thing. Same thing with your father?"

"Not so much. I told him today, and he yelled at me and stormed off." She sipped her coffee and shifted her eyes around the room. She recounted the story of her grandfather and how it had all unfolded. He sat and listened unflinchingly at every troubling detail.

"Maybe he needs more time to process. I'm sure it was a shock to him."

"I've been doing that a lot lately."

"What's that?"

"Shocking people. Hitting them with news they aren't

ready for. Things with my biological mother are starting to work out well, but it hasn't been without its challenges. Her boys don't want anything to do with me. Her husband left her. My mom is still trying to figure out how everyone is supposed to fit into this new thing I created."

Ryan put a hand on her knee. "You didn't create any of this. And it will work out. Things just need time. Look at us." He waved between them as though they'd accomplished something by sharing a cup of coffee.

Her heart sank. Ryan had no idea he was about to join the list of people who she would rock with the truth. She'd considered, and then reconsidered, her decision a hundred times on the ride over. He was already in a tough spot. Would the truth help him, or just free her from the burden she was carrying?

"But sometimes the truth can complicate things," she stuttered out. "People think they want it until they actually hear it. You called me up wanting to know why we broke up. I don't know that you really want to know. Maybe it's better to leave things how they are."

"No," Ryan said, taking her hand in his. The touch wasn't intimate, but she still felt the need to shake free of it. His eyes went wide at her motion. "Is everything all right? You can tell me."

"I don't know if I'm better off this year compared to last year," she admitted. "Part of me is glad I have Leslie and my sister, Kerry. But I look at the ripple effect and wonder if it's all been worth it. Then I wonder if it'll make things worse for you too."

"The truth is always the right way to go." Ryan smiled. "I know I sounded really worked up on the phone. I shouldn't have put that on you. I do want to know more about what happened. I want to understand."

"You're going to be upset." A tear rolled down her cheek and like a hundred times before he quickly swept it away with his thumb.

"Look how much time has passed, Gwen. I've already gone through the mad feelings and the confused feelings. I've moved on. But I don't like how we left things. I don't like not being able to call and check on each other. You were my best friend. And then all the sudden you checked out. You were there, but you weren't. I thought things were good. I thought we were strong. Did I take that for granted? Did I get complacent? Or maybe I was too focused on school and work. I know that I talked a lot about how stressed I was."

She reached over and put her hand on his knee to quiet him. "Ryan, it's not just a saying. When I tell you it wasn't you, it was me, I mean it. I fell apart. Right there in front of you, I disintegrated. My body was still there, but everything inside of me went to dust."

Ryan's eyes blinked hard at her. "I don't understand. What happened? When did that start? I was right there. If I wasn't so distracted with school, I would have seen it."

"I hid it very well. No one knew what was going on with me. You were my best friend too. That's why I didn't want to tell you. My heart was broken, and I thought I would spare you the pain I was feeling."

"What pain?" He drew in his bottom lip, the shadow of tears wetting his nervous green eyes.

"I got pregnant," she whispered, her hand instinctively clutching her stomach. "I was going to wait to tell you. You had so much on your plate, and I thought it was a bad time to drop that bomb on you." She strung her words together quick enough not to have to look up at his reaction. "I knew if I told you at the right time you'd be happy."

"A baby?" he asked, his breath catching in his throat. "I would have been happy any time you told me. You didn't need to keep that from me."

"Right before I was going to surprise you," she sputtered out through sobs, "I had a miscarriage. I went into a tailspin. The idea of being a mother made me look at my own roots completely differently. Then losing hope of finally having someone completely related to me. Someone who was mine in a genetic way I was broken. So many things came crashing down around me, and I tried to hold it together."

"Gwen," Ryan said, disbelief still painting his face. "Gwen. I was right there. We were there together. We were always in things together. Why didn't you tell me? Why didn't you lean on me? I'd have been there for you. I'd have helped you through it."

"It was deeper than anything I could get a grip on. There wouldn't have been anything you could have done to help. I had to find rock bottom."

"I'd have hit it with you."

"And then you wouldn't be here. Look at all you've accomplished in the time we've been apart." She waved around his beautiful apartment. "You were able to finish school. Move out here without waiting for me. You've started a very successful company. If you could see how far I fell, how bad it got, you'd realize I spared you from that."

His expression was angry suddenly. "I didn't ask to be spared from anything. I begged you to tell me what was wrong. I would have stayed. I would have gladly given all this up to have been there for you." His expression softened as she watched him try desperately to process in moments what had taken her over a year to face. "I spent all this time thinking I blew things with you. That I'd let you down or that maybe what we had wasn't the real thing. But it was, wasn't it?"

"It was." She nodded, trying to find the right words. "At some point I had to face the grief and the questions about myself and my adoption. I had to be alone to do that. Because you'd have been compelled to make it better. You'd have been determined to fix it all. That's the kind of man you are. And I'd always been grateful for that. But it wasn't what I needed."

"What do you need now?" He stared at her earnestly.

"I—"

He cut her words short with a kiss. Their kiss. The exact, familiar affectionate love-filled kiss they'd shared for three years. It was so familiar she forgot to pull away. She forgot he was not the man she wanted to kiss. A few beats later, she planted her hand on his chest and pulled back. "I know what I need now, Ryan. I've worked really hard to answer that question."

"You're seeing someone?"

"I might be." It was the best answer she could think to give, but it didn't satisfy him. He kept close, looking ready to kiss her again.

"Might be? How can anyone be with you and be half in? I'm the man you loved for all those years. If it hadn't been for that horrible situation, that loss, we'd still be together. I know that in my heart."

"You need more time to think about everything I told you tonight. You might think you know how you feel about it all, but trust me it comes in waves. And some of those waves will bowl you over."

"I know how I feel. Your biological father will come around. I'll go with you to talk to him tomorrow. He'll have to listen. We'll make sure he does. And Millie and Noel have always been supportive of our relationship. I know they'd be happy for us to be back together."

"Back together?"

"It would feel sudden if we hadn't spent so much time in a relationship before. I know you feel it. What we had was comfortable and right. We know every quirk and every unique thing about each other. We can pick up where we left off."

"Ryan, I know this was a lot of information that I threw at you all at once. Like I said, these truth bombs have been detonating all over the place, and there have been casualties. But we need to slow down here. I live on the other side of the country. I just moved into the old house. I'm starting work in a week."

"I can run my company remotely. I can be wherever you are. Gwen, I still have the ring I was going to propose to you with. I still remember every word I was going to say to you. Nothing has changed."

"I have changed dramatically," she said with a hearty laugh. "And I still have more work to do. You don't have any idea what you're proposing."

As if the word sent him into motion, he was down on one knee in front of her. "Gwen, we can do this. We can pick up where we left off. I never stopped loving you. I will be right by your side through whatever comes. And"—he swallowed back his emotion—"and the child we lost, we can mourn together. And we can try to start a family again."

Gwen blinked hard as though she was hearing or seeing things that weren't there. Was he actually proposing to her? "Ryan, I love you. I really do. But you have to get up off the ground. We're not getting married. We're not back together."

"This makes so much sense, Gwen," he pressed. "You should take some time to think about it. You and I worked. We always did. And we still do."

"I'm not the same person you remember." She tucked her hair away from her face and pulled him up off his knee. "Your life is here."

"Just take some time to think about it, please. That's all I'm asking."

"Fine." The look in his eyes let her know he wouldn't be backing down unless she appeased him. "I'll think about it, but I need to go."

"It's late, you can stay." He gestured at the couch. It was laughable. There was no way he was thinking she'd crash there. It was his bed he wanted her in.

"It's not that late. I'm fine. I have someone waiting for me."

"He's here?" Ryan looked wounded and that only made her more annoyed by the entire situation. He was in no position to be injured by her relationship with anyone else.

"Yes. He's here in California, and he's waiting up for me."

"And you aren't really dating him?"

"That's not something we need to get into, Ryan." She stood with her hand on the doorknob but hesitated to leave. Here she was again, blowing in like a tornado and upending someone else's life. When Ryan had a moment to think about everything she'd told him, he'd find himself in a very valid place of anger. "Ryan, I am so sorry I didn't tell you the truth when it was all happening. You deserved so much more than I gave you. The way I shut down and iced you out, I do regret that. I always will."

"I would have helped you," he said, straightening his glasses that had tipped to the side when he stood. "I still will."

"Goodnight, Ryan. Take some time. Trust me, I've been on this roller coaster a lot longer than you. There will be good days and bad days. And on the bad days I'd imagine you're going to be pretty angry with me."

"I'm never going to be angry with you, Gwen." Ryan tucked his hands back in his pockets and looked down at his shoes. "You were doing the best you could. I should have fought harder for you."

There was some truth to that. Being suddenly unlovable because of her pain was her crime. But letting her go so easily had been his. And that combination spoke volumes about their relationship.

She was in the hallway, heading back down to the car when the tears started flowing freely. Ryan was a good man. They'd shared something she couldn't dismiss easily. And they'd created a child together. They had a love that was almost perfect. A life that almost happened. It was so much easier when a relationship imploded. This one had just quietly slipped through their fingers, like sand they couldn't get a grip on. Hating him would make this easier. But she couldn't bring herself to hate him. He didn't deserve it.

He proposed to her. He was ready, at least in his mind, to completely accept her again. To welcome her back into his life with no hesitation. That was the allure she had to try to stay clear of. The fear of rejection had been so strong lately. Putting herself out there to all these new people was terrifying. There was so much unknown. Her own half-brothers still didn't want to meet her. Her biological father had stormed off upon learning she existed. No matter how solid she tried to make her footing, every rejection distressed her. And now this familiar, loving part of her past was right there in front of her again.

Gwen: I'm on my way
    Griff: All good?
    Gwen: Yup. Just exhausted.
    Griff: Drive careful. See you soon.

She tucked her phone away and put the car in drive. Griff wouldn't pry when she got home. She appreciated that about him. He was persistent in his support, but not pushy in demanding to know everything. There wouldn't be a reason to tell him about the proposal. It wasn't real anyway. Not to her. She put her hands up to her lips where Ryan had kissed her. Where she had let him linger for a moment too long.

It hadn't been anything like the kiss she'd shared with Griff just before she'd left. It wasn't hungry or full of possibility. It was familiar. Ryan was a known commodity.

As well as she knew Griff, there was still plenty they had to discover about each other. Land mines could be waiting under the surface of their feelings.

But there was one thing she knew for sure. And it was all

she needed to know. If she pushed Griff away because she was falling apart, no matter what, he'd still have her back. In whatever capacity she needed him. Even if it meant they couldn't be together. Even if it meant he had to push through her darkest moments. Griff had what Ryan didn't. That hard-to-describe part of his soul that would fight for her. Not fight to have her, but fight for her to be happy. Even if that meant he ended up with less. Whatever that was called, Griff had that. And she had it for him.

Maybe that was love. Real love. Not the love that comes from compatibility or common interests. Not the love that follows the linear path of dating, moving in, marrying, starting a family. The kind of love that takes work, makes no sense on paper, and demands the best from both people. It would be easy to love Ryan. It would be easy to get back on that ride and coast toward the rest of her life.

Coasting just didn't seem like enough anymore.

CHAPTER SEVENTEEN

Mark

It had been ages since he drove with no destination in mind. When he was in his twenties it was his favorite way to clear his head. But he'd gotten too busy since then to meander around in his car. At every intersection he reached, without much thought, he turned whichever way the car seemed to want to go. It didn't matter where he ended up. It didn't matter that he'd been driving for hours and his fuel light had come on. His phone was off. His radio was off. His mind was on.

Leslie had been a tipping point in his life. It was the first time he'd thought he understood love. She was the first woman he could see himself with forever. It wasn't about rescuing her. The circumstances she had found herself in were challenging, but she was busy rescuing herself. That's what he had fallen in love with. He'd casually dated dozens of women since her, but the memories of his time with Leslie hadn't faded.

Then

"You've made huge strides with your production times," Leslie reported with a proud smile. She was in her pajamas, her hair in a messy bun on top of her head. With one foot she rocked Cole in his swing. It was the only thing that would soothe him. The swing had an automatic setting but he, even as a baby, was wise to the difference between that and his mother's rocking rhythm. Stephen had climbed into her lap. Without skipping a beat she shifted the reports in her hand to the side and kept reading. "You'll have a very strong report to give your boss."

"That's thanks to you," Mark said, taking the papers from her hands and tussling Stephen's hair gently. "I still don't know how you do it. You've got these two happy kids and still make time to make me look like a genius at work."

"You've been an angel," Leslie said, reaching out and sliding her hand into his. He never got tired of her touch. "Letting me work from home and covering for me at work has been exactly what I needed to regroup. I've gotten Cole on a decent sleep schedule. I can finally see the bottom of my sink again. It's not constantly covered in yesterday's dishes. I'm ready to go back to work."

"We could make this job last longer." He pulled her hand to his mouth and kissed her delicately. "I have an idea. A pitch that could have us at this a while longer. Maybe a few more months. With these results my boss would be down for just about anything."

"Don't you want to get back to California? This can't possibly be how you want to spend your time." She gestured at their two plates of half-eaten spaghetti on the coffee table in front of them. Paper cups filled with a hundred-dollar bottle of red wine he'd brought her. It wasn't glamorous. But he wanted to tell her it was the happiest he had been in ages. Maybe ever. So much of his life had been about striving to be someone different. Someone more important. Coming home to her tiny apartment at the end of the day and talking work and life over homemade meatloaf, or even sometimes just a bowl of the kids' cereal, had been more fulfilling than any dinner at the fanciest restaurant. Mark wanted to tell her if he never went back to California, he wouldn't care.

"I'm in no rush. California isn't going anywhere." He stood and grabbed the dishes and she stood to join him, but he waved her off. "I've got these. Want to put Cole to bed and then put on that superhero movie?"

"We can't possibly watch that again." She laughed. "It's been a hundred times."

"It makes him so happy. I love when Stephen laughs at the flying scene. That never gets old."

"Mark," Leslie said, as he turned his back to her and headed for the kitchen, the plates balanced in his hands. "Why are you here?"

"It's easier than going back to the hotel. This is where we do our best work. Well, here and the bedroom."

She blushed, strapped Stephen into his bouncy chair and then joined him in the kitchen. "I know we haven't really talked much about what's going on here. I don't want to be that nagging woman who needs to define and label everything."

He'd been too afraid to have this conversation, and he'd been holding his breath, hoping she'd be brave enough to bring it up.

"That's not nagging."

"I just want you to know how much I appreciate all you've done for us. I was in a dark place when we met, and I can't remember the last time I felt this good. You're my hero in so many ways. I just want you to know that. No matter what happens with work or when you go back home. Know that you've changed my life." She covered her face with her hand and groaned. "Never mind, I'm bumbling this badly. I know you're this consummate bachelor who loves his life. I just felt like it was important for you to know how you saved me."

He put the dishes on the counter and pulled her into his arms. "Leslie, you've done far more for me than I've done for you. You and the boys are exactly what I needed. I love coming back here at the end of the day. There is nowhere else I'd rather be."

"But eventually you're going to have to be somewhere else. I just don't want you to feel beholden to us. I see this for what it is."

"What do you think this is?"

"It's a stop on a very long journey for you. A journey that's going to take you to many different places. I know you can't stay, but I want you to know I'm glad you've stayed as long as you have. The boys adore you. I adore you. But I don't want you to feel trapped. If you make this job longer than it needs to be just because you're worried about us, I'll feel awful. Don't feel bad for us."

"I've never felt bad for you," he corrected quickly. "You're one of the strongest women I've ever known. You needed a break, not pity. I'm not here because of that. And I'm not considering making the job longer because of that either."

"So then why?"

He nearly told her he loved her. Because he knew without a doubt he did. But he was terrified he'd scare her off. Change things and end up losing her. "I'm here because I want to be. I want to stay, because I'm very happy. I like the spaghetti. I like the kids' movies and the silly belly laughs. And you, I can't seem to get enough of you." He brushed her bangs off her forehead and kissed her passionately. It was a kiss that would, like most nights, have led to more. But there was a little cry from the baby in the other room.

"I'm going to put him to bed," she whispered, reluctantly pulling away from Mark. "Will you put the tape in of that horrible superhero movie?"

"You've got it. After I get these dishes washed."

"You are too good to be true." She disappeared into the living room to sort the boys out.

He squirted some soap onto the sponge and got to work on the dinner plates. How could this be the place he felt most like himself? After all the work he'd done to climb the corporate ladder and be successful, standing here doing these dishes made his heart full. Because while he did these dishes, he knew Leslie was busy rocking her chubby-cheeked child to sleep. That was what made him happiest. Anything he could do to give her time with her children was an accomplishment more rewarding than any promotion he'd gotten at work.

Less than an hour later Stephan had fallen asleep, resting against Mark's shoulder. How could anyone have left these children for some job overseas? With his sailboat pajamas and cheeks made rosy by sleep, Stephen snuggled against Mark as he carried him to bed. This was a life he could live. These were the people he could live it with.

Mark's car sputtered to a stop under the bright gas station lights and he counted himself lucky. He was in the middle of nowhere, and if he hadn't made it to this gas station, he'd have been stuck. Cell service was spotty at best. He filled his tank and pulled up his GPS. It was time to head back home. He needed answers. If this girl Gwen really was his daughter, it meant Leslie had known the child was his and given it up for adoption without a word to him. There were little avenues in his brain he would start to go down and then stop suddenly. He was fighting the urge to make excuses for her. There had been something out of their control that had broken them apart. That wasn't her fault. But they'd agreed that when things cooled down they would get in touch. By the time they talked again, she was already considering making things work with Paul. Did he know about the baby? Had he forced her to give the girl up for adoption? The very idea of it made him boil with anger.

When he made his way back to familiar roads and reliable cell service he called Jocelyn. This was too big to sort out on his own. He didn't want to involve any of his other friends just yet. Not before he knew more about what had happened, and what still might happen. But Jocelyn could help.

Likely because of the urgency in his voice, Jocelyn invited him over to her place without hesitation. Before they were even settled into her living room he was recounting all that had happened.

"I think we should open some wine," Jocelyn said as Mark launched into his feelings regarding Gwen. She planted her hand on his chest and calmed him. "This is heavy stuff."

"I know."

"This is the woman you were telling me about before? The one with kids who broke your heart?" She uncorked the wine and filled two glasses.

"Yes."

"You're saying she had your child and didn't tell you?"

"And gave that child up for adoption. At some point she reconciled with her husband too. That ass probably forced her to choose."

"What was Gwen like?" Jocelyn asked, filling his wine-glass nearly to the brim.

"I don't know. I yelled at her and then ran off."

"Ouch."

"Yes, not my finest moment. I'm having quite a few of those failures lately. I just couldn't believe what she was telling me."

"I'm sure she'll understand that."

"You say that is if we're going to talk again. I don't know if she'll want to, or what she wants at all."

"You think she's really your daughter?"

"I do." He wasn't sure if it was the resemblance to his mother, or the resemblance to Leslie, probably the combination of both. But he knew she was telling the truth.

"Then you'll figure out what to do. This girl didn't decide what was going to happen to her. She didn't get a choice.

Now she's putting herself out there, and the last things she wants to be is rejected."

"I didn't mean to make her feel that way." His shoulders hunched as he took the wine and drank three large sips.

"She'll understand I'm sure." Jocelyn rubbed his back. "What I don't understand is how this Leslie woman kept this from you. Did you just never talk again or something?"

"I told you we were working together. My firm hired her as a consultant. She was having a hard time at home and I made some accommodations to help. Not because I felt bad for her, but because she was that talented. I wanted to work with her, and I figured she'd be most productive if she could have some flexibility with her kids."

"And then you fell for her?"

"Hard."

"And then the work was over?"

"Yes. Well, not quite. It was mostly over, and I was going to invent some more so we could keep doing what we were doing. I wasn't ready for it to be over. Actually I never wanted it to be over. But Leslie got called in by her boss. Someone had made an accusation that she and I were having an inappropriate relationship."

"Which you were," Jocelyn pointed out.

"Yes. But she was going to bear the brunt of the repercussions. My company had hired hers to do work for us. She had a responsibility to guard our proprietary information. She was the one who would lose everything. My company was more lax, and I'd just saved them a small fortune by implementing the work Leslie had done."

"What happened?"

"Leslie denied the relationship, but they weren't

convinced. So I went into the office and fell on the sword. I told them that I'd been pressuring and harassing Leslie the entire time we were working together. She'd been thwarting my advances, but I had been relentlessly pursuing her. I told them that Leslie had been nothing but professional, even covering up my behavior as to preserve the relationship between our companies. She'd endured my harassment for their sake."

"Whoa, that was a ballsy move." Jocelyn looked impressed.

"Was it though? We're talking more than twenty-six years ago. Guys were getting away with that kind of crap every day and I knew it. I got a slap on the wrist at work and had to go through some sexual harassment training. I actually think my next two promotions were because I was seen as one of the boys, not despite that. But the hard part was, Leslie and I had to break things off. I'd woven a story, and at least for a little while, we had to cool it. She was sure work was monitoring her company phone. People at work were watching her closely. My office wanted me back in California immediately. We agreed we'd let things cool off and then figure something out. I told her the day I left for the airport that I loved her and I was sorry this had happened."

"Did she say she loved you too?" Jocelyn was on the edge of her seat as though she were watching a fascinating movie.

"I think so."

"You think so?"

"I don't know for sure. I've tried to replay that in my mind over and over. She said she cared for me. She was grateful. She couldn't imagine I wouldn't be waking up with her tomorrow. But I don't know if she said she loved me."

"And by the time things calmed down she was back with her husband?"

"She was at least talking to him again. Something drastic had changed by the next time we talked a couple of months later."

"I'd say something changed. She was pregnant with your child."

"It was as if what we had never existed to her. She was very matter of fact about everything. She had this kind of resolve as though she was just determined to move forward and not back."

"And you were heartbroken."

"I really was."

"And she went on to have your baby."

"It seems that way."

"I can't even imagine what you are feeling right now. Anger? Sadness?"

"Confusion," he admitted. "I just don't understand why. And the only thing I can think is that she didn't love me. I pictured our lives together. If she'd have told me she was pregnant, I'd have been all in. It all would have started right then."

"Things would certainly be different for you."

"I just want to know why."

"Your daughter, Gwen, might have those answers."

"I have a daughter," he whispered, putting his wineglass down before he dropped it. "I'm a father."

"Congratulations?" Jocelyn said, half question, half proclamation. "Now what? Do you have a way to get in touch with Gwen?"

"I'm sure she'll be by my father's bedside again tomorrow.

But I need to talk to Leslie first. Gwen shouldn't have to answer for her mother. A mother she didn't even know. I want to hear it from Leslie first."

"Do you know how to get in touch with her?"

"I've found her on social media before. Her account is set to private so I can only see her profile picture. I never felt like it was right to burst back into her life. I thought everything we had connecting us was in the past." He pulled up her information and began typing a message.

"What are you writing?" Jocelyn asked, leaning over his shoulder and sounding alarmed. He'd launched into a list of questions he was demanding answers to, but then promptly erased them. Instead he wrote his phone number and a single message.

We need to talk.

CHAPTER EIGHTEEN

Gwen

Griff was still in the hotel lobby sipping on a fresh drink when she returned. His eyes looked worried, but he still plastered on a smile. "You doing all right?" he asked, patting the stool next to him. She wanted to go upstairs. She wanted to crawl under the thick down comforter in the bed and pull it up over her head. Instead, she sat by him and rested her head on his shoulder.

"I'm doing all right."

"Did you decide to tell him?"

"I did." She sighed loudly. "It was the right thing to do. He was a part of something. He was the father to that child. I feel like he deserves the same right to grieve as I've had. I told myself I was protecting him from that. But really I was just protecting myself."

"How did he take it?"

"I think he was in shock. At some point the anger is going to set in. And that's fair. I lied to him and pushed him away."

"You're hard to get angry with. Plus I'm sure he understands what an emotional thing it was for you to go through."

"And now, in some ways he'll go through it too. And that's on top of this new breakup."

"Bummer," Griff said, putting an arm over her.

"Don't be petty," she said. "It doesn't suit you."

"You're right. I do hope things work out for him. I'm just glad you came back here tonight."

"You thought I wouldn't?" She leaned away from him and checked his expression for some sign of his worry.

"I thought there was a chance. You and Ryan were together for a long time. You went through something very difficult. That can make for some dynamic situations."

"Nothing dynamic. Trust me. I just needed to face that and close that door. It was time."

"And it's closed?"

"Shut tight."

He kissed the crown of her head. "So about what I said before you left. Are we going to take this leap or keep talking ourselves out of it?"

"I think I need to see those charts you made," Gwen teased. "Are there any that cover who gets control of the television on which night?"

"We should go to bed," he whispered, sliding his hand into hers.

"I'm ready for bed."

Something was suddenly different between them, and

she welcomed it. Whatever they decided to do tonight, and every day after that, was a choice they'd make together. Things were about to change, and she was ready. They had been smart about it. Thoughtful and reserved. But love couldn't be stopped. Not a love like theirs.

CHAPTER NINETEEN

Mark

Video chat felt impersonal but it was the best he could think of. Typing out his questions to Leslie wasn't satisfying enough. Even a regular phone call wouldn't do justice to the situation. He wanted to be able to see her face when she explained, or tried to explain, what had happened.

It was early on the West Coast but he couldn't imagine waiting any longer. It had already been decades of time wasted.

He'd showered and combed his hair. Shaved and put on a good shirt. He sat in his office, thick volumes of important books became the backdrop as his video call connected.

"Mark," Leslie said, her hands covering her mouth as her quivering chin peeked out. She looked remarkably unchanged by time. Obviously they'd both aged, but so much of her was the same. Distractingly so. Seeing her, even just on the screen of his laptop, was like stepping through time. The old hurt was there, but so was the affection he felt for her. When Leslie's hand finally came down from her face he saw her sweet lips and he instantly remembered the best kiss he'd ever had. It was their first kiss.

"Hello, Leslie." His voice shook, but he quickly cleared his throat. Behind Leslie was a wall of family photographs. Had she given as much thought to where she'd sit for this call? Did she want him to see how much her life had changed over the years?

"Oh my gosh, I don't know what to say. I'm so sorry." Her tears smudged her makeup, but he was determined not to be moved by them. Something terrible had happened here, and he wanted answers. Seeing her again made his head spin. Her pleas for forgiveness were compelling. And he wanted to tell her it was all fine. But nothing about this was. He reached past his nostalgia and gripped his anger, yanking it back toward the front of his mind.

"I'm not looking for apologies, Leslie. I want to know what happened."

Leslie wiped at her eyes and didn't flinch at his harsh words. Instead, she pulled herself together and sat up straighter. "I don't know where to start. Have you met Gwen?"

"It didn't go well. I was blindsided." He sat back in his large leather chair and rubbed a hand over his forehead.

Leslie hummed knowingly. "You still do that when you're stressed?" She mirrored his movement with his hand. "Gwen is a very understanding woman. I'm sure it'll be all right."

"I'll fix it with Gwen. I just needed time. I didn't want to try to get answers out of her that should be coming from you."

"That fair," Leslie sputtered out. "She's a wonderful girl. Amazing, really. She was raised by two very special people. They have two boys of their own. A very happy family overall."

"I guess we got lucky there." Saying *we*, as it related to their child, felt more like a barb than anything unifying. He felt robbed. Robbed of time and of having a choice in any of this. "Leslie, why didn't you tell me you were pregnant? I would have stayed. We could have figured it out."

"I didn't know I was pregnant when things were happening at work. I was so afraid I was going to lose my job because of what you and I had done. I wasn't a rule breaker, and then all of the sudden I'm in my boss's office being told I could be fired if I had done anything inappropriate with you."

"I fixed that. It was handled."

"For you it was. But that followed me around. Everyone knew the truth, and the scrutiny was killing me. I was still married. Paul and I were separated, but by law he was my husband. You could just move on to the next job and the next woman, but for me it was life-altering when we got caught."

"There was no next woman. I guess that's the part I don't understand. Did you know I was ready to start a life with you? Maybe I wasn't clear enough. You and the boys, that was the life I wanted."

She leaned away from the camera until she was nearly out of the frame. Her hair swept down in front of her eyes and he was so glad they weren't meeting in person. He'd have been powerless against the urge to reach out and brush her hair away. The slump of her shoulders would have him pulling her into his arms. The distance was a gift.

"Mark—"

"Did you know that?" He pressed on, asking for the only answer that mattered to him. Did she know he loved her? Did she know he wanted to be with her?

"I think I did know." She drew in a deep breath and touched the screen as if to reach out and touch him. "I think I've spent a lot of years trying to convince myself what you and I had was a fling. Because a fling ends, and it isn't something you pine over. It's not something you spend the rest of your life comparing everything to. I had to make what we had feel small, so it didn't cast a shadow on the rest of my life."

"That day in the airport, when I told you I loved you, did you say it back? I can't remember now." He rested his chin in his hand and leaned in. He'd remembered most of their time together vividly, but their goodbye wasn't as clear.

She closed her eyes for a moment and smiled. "I did say it back. I told you that I loved you and you saved me. Letting go of your hand for the last time, it was like letting go of a part of myself. I didn't know I was pregnant then. I didn't know I'd be getting back with Paul. I just knew you were leaving and I'd miss you terribly."

"Did you think then, when the work stuff blew over, we'd be together? Did you ever think you and I had a chance? Because I did."

"That day at the airport, I wasn't expecting you to say you loved me. I really kept telling myself you were too good to be true. Everything you were doing had to be out of pity. I kept bracing myself, worrying the last time I saw you would be the last time." She was speaking quickly, moving her hand around animatedly as she tried to explain.

"How could you think that? I was right there with you every night. I adored the boys. Didn't you see that?"

"Yes. I was afraid. I knew I'd fallen in love with you and it was like I was clutching ice in my hands. You'd melt eventually. It would all go away, just like it did with Paul."

"I'm nothing like Paul," Mark snapped.

"I know that," she breathed out, sounding defeated. "Trust me I know the difference between you."

"Why didn't you call me when you found out you were pregnant with my child?" His teeth were grinding together as he braced for an explanation he knew wouldn't satisfy him. There would be nothing she could say that would be enough.

After a moment of searching for the right words, Leslie did her best. "It's amazing what we can convince ourselves of. I was sure you had moved on. How could a man like you want a life like mine? I just kept telling myself that over and over again. I thought of myself and my family as a burden to you."

"I never did anything to make you feel that way, did I?" His chest burned with regret and anxiety.

"Not a thing. You did everything right. I wasn't accustomed to that kind of treatment. I didn't trust it. I was young and overwhelmed. And Paul . . . he was calling again. I left work because of all the drama between you and me. I didn't want people to notice I was pregnant. They would figure out it was yours. Even from overseas, Paul started helping out more financially so that I could stop working. He thought it would be better if I weren't working. He always felt that way and suddenly he got what he wanted. Being home, Paul still being gone, I became very isolated."

"Did he make you give her up?" Rage rippled through his body as he held his breath and waited for the answer.

She blinked slow and then dropped her eyes downward.

"I never told him either." Leslie shook her head, as if gravely disappointed in herself. "He stayed overseas until after I had Gwen. The boys were so small they didn't remember. I've kept this all to myself for all these years."

"You never told Paul? All these years married and you never told him you had my child? Did he know about me?"

"We both decided," she paused and made a disgusted noise. "No, he decided we should just act like the time we spent apart never happened. I'm sure he wasn't over there honoring our vows. It was easier just to play pretend. Most of our marriage worked like that."

"And then Gwen came knocking on your door?" He was willing to give a shred of understanding at how life altering that would have been for Leslie. It was certainly turning his world upside down. "That's how Paul found out?"

"Yes. After I heard from Gwen, I told Paul the truth. He asked me to choose. I was either going to cover this up and get a lawyer to keep Gwen out of our lives, or he was going to leave."

"You chose Gwen?" Mark couldn't help the way his lips turned up slightly and his eyes brightened. That must have been an impossibly hard choice, but Leslie could handle difficult things.

"Yes, I chose to have Gwen in my life even if that meant my marriage fell apart. I'm going to say something now that maybe I shouldn't." She wiped at her nose and cleared her throat.

"We used to be pretty blunt with each other. I want to hear whatever you have to say."

"Mark, I had a good life. My children are still processing things right now but being with Paul afforded them pros-

perity and security with their father around. I made it work."
She paused, still looking unsure if she could manage to speak
the words. "I should have picked you. You were a better man
in every way, and I would have been lucky to have shared a
life with you. Gwen could have had her father. I could have
had a man who understood and valued me. Sometimes it's
better the devil you know. Paul was the easiest option. He
made sense on paper. But by saying all of that, I could hurt
Kerry badly."

"Kerry?" Mark racked his brain for the name to bring him
some kind of recognition, but it didn't.

Leslie gulped. Of everything she'd said so far this looked
like the hardest to get out. "Paul and I had another daughter
years later."

"After you gave up Gwen?" He didn't bother hiding his
judgment. "You had another child?"

"Yes. And Kerry is one of the best things that ever
happened to me. If I'd have chosen another path, she
wouldn't exist. It's why I pushed away the idea that being
with you would have been an option. I had to eliminate that
from my mind, otherwise I'd have spent my life comparing
what we had to what I was actually living. And I would have
gone mad."

"This is a lot to take in. I don't know what to tell you. I
feel—" There didn't seem any words strong enough to
explain.

Leslie twisted the bracelet on her left wrist and it
reminded him of their time together years ago. So much had
changed, but a few small things still tethered them to the
past. "I'm sure this doesn't need to be said, but none of this is
Gwen's fault. Whatever kind of anger you have for me, it's

not hers to carry. She really is a lovely girl. Smart. And I couldn't help but notice all the little things she does that remind me of you. I don't know what you have going on or how complicated it will be to integrate her into your life, but I hope you find a way. I lost Paul over it, and Cole and Stephen haven't really spoken to me. I know that can be daunting. She's worth it."

"I never married or had children." His eyes darted away. He'd never regretted his choice, but telling Leslie that he hadn't ever taken the plunge felt somehow as though he hadn't met his potential. "Gwen is not going to disrupt anything. I'm retired now. I've got nothing but time to get to know her, if that's what she wants. I didn't make a very good first, or second, impression."

"She's very understanding. Thank goodness for that." Leslie drew in a deep breath. "I know you don't want my apologies, but I truly am sorry. I made a choice that at the time felt best for my boys, for Gwen, and for everyone else involved. Now, I realize that part of my choice was very self-ish. I wish I'd given you the opportunity to know her or at least know about her. I knew you cared about me and the boys. I should have trusted that. All our lives would be much different now."

"We won't ever know," Mark admitted somberly. "We could have screwed it all up too. But I would have liked a shot at finding out. What we had, it was something special."

"It really was," Leslie agreed. "I have to live with the aftermath of my choices. That hasn't been easy."

"I won't make it harder for you than it already is."

"Where do we go from here?" Leslie nibbled on her thumbnail, and he was transported back to her ratty couch in her tiny apartment. She was every bit the same woman he'd fallen in love with.

"We have a daughter." The words were thick and unfamiliar on his tongue. "I'm a dad. I don't know how to be a dad."

"You did great with my boys when they were little. You're going to do amazing with Gwen."

"She already has parents. I don't want to overstep. I'm sure this is a lot for them too."

"They're sweet. Millie and Noel Fox. They've been very welcoming to me and Kerry. Gwen's brothers, Dave and Nick, are great too."

"How old is Kerry?" It was strange to think of Leslie with another child. If he was honest, all of this was strange but at least they were talking.

"Kerry's eighteen. She's leaving for college soon and frankly I'm devastated. With everything else going on, I've been a bit of a mess. I'm going to throw myself back into my career. I've put it on hold for so long."

"If you raised her, she's more than ready to go off to college."

"Oh, she's ready. She can't wait. It's me who isn't sure what life is going to look like once she's gone. That's why work will be my distraction."

"I was wondering what you decided to do for work. You were always so impressive."

"I didn't do half of what I wanted to. Now's my time though. Paul is gone. The kids will be living their own lives. Kerry is going to be in California. Paul was tough on her, tough on all the kids. So she wanted some distance. She's thinking med school. Paul doesn't know yet. He's not going to like that."

"I'm sensing a theme with Paul."

"You'd be right. But it's her father and I know she is just trying to balance what he wants and what she wants for herself. Kerry is strong, stronger than me. She'll do fine."

"You know I'm still here in California. I can check in on her when you need it. I have lots of time on my hands now that I'm retired."

"Lots of time on your hands? I doubt that. I know you're not married, but surely you're not single. I always imagined how lucky a woman who ended up with you would be." She blushed. "You don't have to answer that."

"No, it's all right. I'm single at the moment, but I've just met a lovely woman named Jocelyn. She's been helping me get through some things. But she's coming out of a relationship so we're just spending time together. Commiserating, really."

"She's helping you get through things? These things?" Leslie waved a hand as though she was his biggest cause of stress. He wished there was only one thing weighing him down.

"My father is in hospice. He doesn't have long to live. Gwen found him first, apparently thinking it was me. But then she realized he was her grandfather."

"I'm so sorry to hear that."

"I haven't gone to see him. I haven't seen him since I was in my twenties. If it weren't for Gwen, I wouldn't be considering it."

"But you're considering it now?"

"I know Gwen wants me to. I'm worried what she'll think

of me if I can't man up and just go." He looked at Leslie for advice. She'd been doing this parenting thing for a long time. Surely she'd have the answer.

"Guilt from kids is not a reason to do anything. I'm in no position to give you advice. But parenting, when you're doing it right, usually ends up with them at least a little mad or disappointed in you."

"Then I'm off to a great start." He smiled and when Leslie smiled back his heart sang. That was the biggest goal of his life many years ago. Making her smile.

A silence stretched between them, and Mark wondered for a minute if the connection on the video chat had frozen. Finally Leslie broke the quiet.

"Thank you, Mark. Honestly. Thank you for being even moderately understanding. I know you're angry, and you have every right to be. I don't expect that to just go away. But the fact that you are willing to have a conversation with me just reminds me of the kind of man you are. I was lucky to know you. And Gwen will be lucky to have you."

"We should try to talk again soon. Maybe I'll come out that way to meet Millie and Noel some time."

"That would be wonderful." Leslie lit with a mix of excitement and relief. It still did something to him. Her happiness was inexplicably linked to his. To know he was making some of her ache lessen just a bit lifted his spirits. "Do you have a way to get in touch with Gwen?"

"I know where she's going to be. It's probably the best place I can meet her right now anyway. My father doesn't have much time left. I need to either see him or live with the consequences of missing the chance."

"Good luck. I know you'll do what's best."

They said their goodbyes and he closed his laptop. He couldn't call this phase of his life boring anymore. It was amazing how that resolve to steer clear of his father had melted away. It seemed far less important to hold his grudge. The simple realization that there was a child in this world that was his, was powerful. Everything else seemed to fall away.

CHAPTER TWENTY

Gwen

Markus was asleep again when she and Griff arrived in the morning. The nurse informed them he'd had a bad night. Lots of pain. The best thing they could do now was keep him comfortable.

"Maybe we shouldn't stay today," Gwen suggested, hanging out in the doorway instead of taking her normal seat. "I don't want to disturb him."

"And are you also trying to avoid Mark?" Griff asked, tugging her gently inside. "This would be where he'd come if he wanted to talk."

"And this would be where he didn't come if he didn't want anything to do with me. I'm not worried about him showing up. I'm worried about sitting here all day and he doesn't. If I'm not here, I'll never know."

Griff opened his arms and she stepped into them. "We

should stay for a bit. Even though Markus is sleeping, I feel like he'll know we're here."

The light knock on the door behind them made her heart thump. She didn't want to turn her face only to find out it wasn't Mark.

"Gwen?" the voice asked in a whisper.

It was him.

She turned her face but kept her cheek resting on Griff's chest. She wasn't ready to let him go yet. Maybe Mark was just here to argue again.

"Can we talk for a minute in the hallway?"

Griff straightened up. "Or maybe get a cup of coffee in the cafeteria. It's delicious."

"It's not," Gwen said apologetically. "He's kidding."

Mark gave a half laugh before his eyes moved over his father's sleeping face. Falling very still, he stood there for a moment staring.

"We could stay in here," Gwen suggested. "He's sleeping. The pain was getting bad. They've sedated him."

"Ah. Well—" Mark wrung his hands together nervously.

"Or the hallway," Gwen said with a smile, walking toward him and gesturing out the door. He followed and looked relieved.

Gwen tucked her hair back and wondered if that made her look more like her grandmother. "I didn't mean to imply yesterday that you had to come see your dad. I don't know the whole story. It wasn't my place to try to pressure you."

"You don't have to apologize for anything," Mark said, waving his hands animatedly. "I have to apologize. We've met twice now, and I've really blown it. This is a lot to take in. Then add on my dad's situation. I was not handling it well."

"I understand." She bit at her lip, unsure of what else to say. "I didn't want to come here and spring this on you. Trust me, I went back and forth plenty of times on whether I was really going to come out to California."

"I'm glad you did. I talked with Leslie this morning."

"You did?"

"Yes, we had a video call."

"How did that go?" She took a lock of her hair and wrapped it nervously around her finger. Her one-woman-wrecking-crew was back in action and she worried she'd caused them to fight.

"It went good, actually. I'm not saying I understand why she did what she did. But we talked, and we're going to keep talking."

"Did you love her?" Gwen blurted out.

"I did. I really loved her."

"It seems silly. People have children all the time and the circumstances are always different. I just wondered if I was made with love in mind."

"You were." He smiled. "But we all went on to have the lives we were meant to. I believe that. I don't want to spend too much of my time wondering what it would have been like if Leslie had told me about you and we'd stayed together. I don't think it will be good for me to go there. I'd like to focus on now."

"Now?"

"I'm a father all of a sudden."

"You don't have other kids?" She watched his face closely as he answered.

"No. After Leslie and I went our separate ways I wrote

off the idea that I could give enough to someone to be a parent."

"You missed my moody teenage years. I don't need very much right now. I've got great parents. A promising career, I hope. I'm not really looking for anything except to know you."

"I can handle that." He smiled and fidgeted around with his car keys in his pocket.

"You want to leave, don't you?"

"I don't like hospitals much. It's not that I don't want to spend more time with you. I do. Would you and Griff want to come back to my place for dinner? I have some friends I'd like you to meet. I'm sure you'll be heading back East soon."

"We need to leave in a couple days. I'm worried about Markus though." She looked over her shoulder into his room.

"I'll make sure he's not alone. I don't know if it'll be me in there with him or a friend, but he won't be alone."

Gwen nodded. "Dinner tonight sounds good. "

"Do you have any allergies or anything? What's your favorite dish? Oh, and dessert."

"Mark, we've got a lot of catching up to do. We don't have to do it all at once. Whatever you make will be fine. Though I don't like mushrooms."

"I hate them," Mark boomed.

His enthusiasm was warming her heart. "I must get that from you."

CHAPTER TWENTY-ONE

Mark

It was terribly last-minute but his former assistant Jane and her daughters were so excited they had agreed to come by for dinner.

The news had been hard to share at first. There was no good way to start the story. He couldn't just blurt out that he had a daughter he hadn't known about. And he couldn't get so far down into the story that he explained the complex relationship he had with Leslie. But that was the nice thing about friends; you didn't have to make the perfect presentation. They'd wade through the words and the clumsy delivery and find the same joy at the core of the story that he was trying to portray.

Jocelyn's invitation had been a little trickier. It had only been a week since they'd met. But she'd been involved in this. She'd heard all the details and given him sound advice. And more than that, she was lovely. She'd make a nice addition around the table. If the conversation lagged, he could count on her to keep things going.

The meal had come together nicely. His Italian recipes were his most reliable, and so far he had it all timed perfectly. When the doorbell rang he was relieved to see it was Jocelyn.

"It smells amazing in here," she said in a singsong voice as she handed over a bottle of white wine. In her other hand she held the string to an oversized balloon that said: *New Dad!*

"Very cute."

"Congratulations. I'm looking forward to meeting her."

"It's not too weird? I feel like I'm putting you in a strange position. I don't know how this is going to go. It could be a disaster."

"I had no idea when I called you over in the parking lot to jump-start my car that I'd be getting my own front-row seat to a reality television show."

"I'm glad I could give you some entertainment. I was complaining about things being too boring when we met."

"That changed quickly."

"It sure did."

She grabbed a wooden spoon and lifted the lid on the saucepan simmering on the stove. Stirring it, she glanced at him over her shoulder. "Did you talk with Leslie?"

He wasn't sure if she was a little jealous or just curious. Either way, he was glad she'd asked. "I did. We did a video chat this morning."

"Was it love at first sight again?" Tapping the sauce off the spoon, she set it down and turned toward him with a wry smile.

"It was strange to see her again. All of this is happening

fast. But no, Leslie and I are very different people now than we were years ago. That's a door I've closed tight."

"Never say never." She wagged her finger at him. "That kind of love, the way you talked about her, doesn't just go away. Is she still married?"

"Getting divorced."

Jocelyn hummed. "Really? Very interesting."

"She lied to me about carrying my child and giving her up for adoption. That's something I don't think anyone could come back from."

"It was a betrayal for sure. I'm just saying, even if you close that door don't lock it."

"Are you my new matchmaker?"

"I can be," Jocelyn said, clapping her hands together with excitement. "You're a very eligible bachelor. It wouldn't be hard to find you someone."

"You weren't kidding about not wanting to date. I get the hint."

"It wasn't a hint," she teased. "I was pretty blunt, actually. I thought that was your deal too."

"It was."

"Was?"

"Is. I don't know. I'm in emotional overload right now. Don't listen to me. Just help me make the garlic bread and pretend this isn't going to be a disaster of a dinner."

"It's going to be great," she said, rubbing a hand over his back. "You have a daughter."

"A daughter I know nothing about."

"How fun is that? You get to learn everything about her. You get to spend time getting to know her. That's exciting."

"How do you stay so positive all the time?"

"Therapy, wine, and good friends."

"I hope I can count myself in that company. I feel like I'm going to need some friends."

Gwen and Griff arrived twenty minutes later. This time they came straight to the side door. He held a bottle of Scotch and she had a tiny bouquet of flowers.

"You didn't need to bring anything," he said, ushering them in and introducing them to Jocelyn. She took the flowers and rummaged through the kitchen until she found a vase to put them in. She'd started making herself comfortable in his space.

"Thank you for having us," Gwen said stiffly. Griff reached over and put his hand on the small of her back. It was a simple gesture, but Mark watched as it infused her with a jolt of relief.

Jane and her girls were knocking at the door a moment later. The house was suddenly filled with joyful squealing and exchanging introductions and hugs. Griff moved toward Mark and grinned. "We're outnumbered."

"I should have done the math better," Mark chuckled. "Hopefully they don't gang up on us."

"I'm sure they will." Griff leaned against the kitchen counter, and Mark could feel his scrutinizing appraisal.

"How long have you and Gwen been together?"

"Formally?" Griff looked at his watch. "About thirty-two hours."

"Really?"

"We grew up together," Griff explained. "At the end of last year she was struggling, trying to decide if she wanted to find you and Leslie. I'd lost my job, and we got close again after not seeing each other for years. It's been a whirlwind, and we kept trying to convince ourselves it would be a bad idea to start dating until things settle down."

"Things never settle down." Mark chuckled knowingly. "But I guess thirty-two hours ago you came to the same conclusion."

"Exactly."

"I'm glad she's had someone with her while she's been dealing with all of this."

"She has a lot of people," Griff explained. "She hit the lottery with her adoptive family. They're amazing. But it's still been tough. Gwen's had some other stuff going on too. I'm sure at some point she'll tell you all about it."

"You know her well?"

"I do," Griff replied proudly.

"Any advice for me?" Mark tapped his fingers on the counter. "I could use any help I can get."

"Gwen's searching."

"For more family?" Mark asked. He was anxious to connect her with his sisters and their children. He could imagine the loud party that would warrant.

"She's searching for herself. For what makes her unique. For what connects her to those things and those stories. She knows she's part of the Fox family. She knows she looks like Leslie and your mother. Who made her strong? Who made her smart and driven? Where does it all come from? All the strange and wonderful things that make her who she is. That's going to be your job."

"And what's your job?" Mark asked, already feeling protective of Gwen and grilling this boy about his intentions.

"My job is to remind her every day that, no matter what she finds or where she finds it, she's already all of those things."

CHAPTER TWENTY-TWO

Gwen

The week had been filled with surprises. The biggest of which was how much she genuinely liked Mark. They'd gotten off on the wrong foot. That was obvious. But when she took a step back and listened to him talk about his life it made more sense. She had no right to expect him to go see his father. No right to guilt him into it.

Dinner with his friends had felt comfortable, which she counted as a win. There was an abundance of laughter and endless questions being traded for answers. Mark and Griff had hit it off, aligning as the only men around the table that evening. A few times, when talk turned to old stories where they were the punch line, that alliance proved necessary.

After dinner and dessert, Mark had invited them all down to the pier on the lake. The air was warm and he'd set chairs out for everyone. Jane's girls had opted to kick their shoes off and dunk their feet in while everyone else basked under the glow of the tiki torches Mark had affixed to the poles of the pier. The moon was nearly full and Gwen imagined her mother and father at their new condo. They'd be asleep by this time of night. Asleep under that same giant moon.

Mark opened up a small plastic table and Jane had carried down some plastic cups on a tray. They were filled with ice and silly little umbrellas.

"What are these?" Gwen asked, trying to eye the pitcher Mark placed on the table. The drink was a bright yellow concoction with fruit floating across the top.

Mark lit with pride as he gestured down toward the drink. "It's Limon Granizado." Gwen loved hearing her father pronounce things with a Spanish accent. She'd always wondered what made her skin darker than her parents'. What part of the world should she identify with? Now she had that answer and she was excited to learn more. Four years of Spanish in high school had left her with mostly the ability to ask where the library was or tell someone the weather.

Mark continued to explain as he filled the glasses. "This is my mother's recipe." He paused. "Your grandmother's recipe. We never had air-conditioning when I was growing up but we had a lemon tree in the yard. She'd make these after dinner. It's a slushy kind of drink. You're supposed to crush the ice in a blender but we never had that either. You put the ice in a bag and just beat it up for a while. All of us kids used to love that part. Smashing the bag with the rolling pin or hitting it on the ground outside."

Jane laughed as she held out her glass. "Is that what you did?"

"No," Mark admitted. "I used the blender. Mom would understand." He filled each glass and handed them out as the conversation turned to questions about his mother.

The drink was delicious and Gwen felt a connection spark in her. This was a family recipe. Something that other people in her bloodline had created and enjoyed together. The lake was still and calm as their laughter rolled across it into the night sky. The pier was alive with their joy and no one looked more pleased with that than Mark as he took a seat by Gwen.

"This drink is really good. Thank you for making it and for having us over. I'm sure that you weren't expecting this and I am sorry if I've caught you off guard." He looked down at her nearly empty glass and leaned over for the pitcher.

"Please don't apologize to me about coming into my life. You can't imagine how I was feeling just a few weeks ago. I think your timing is impeccable."

"How were you feeling?" She asked, visually tracing the lines around his eyes as they grew deeper. A flash of worry bolted through her as she wondered if he was sick.

"I've had a very full life. A busy life. Then all the sudden it all changed. I bought this house and pretended that maybe all I ever wanted was to sit on that porch and sip on a drink and look out at this lake."

"That sounds pretty nice." She plastered on a smile in spite of how sad he looked.

"Careful," he warned. "That's what they want you to think. They want you to believe you work hard your whole life so one day you can slow down, almost to a stop. I fell for that. And now look at my glass."

She looked at the cup in his hand and then back at him. "Is this a glass half full kind of thing?"

"No," he chuckled. "The ice has no time to melt. I was sitting up there not too long ago watching the ice melt in my drink. That was my excitement. Now here we are, late into the night. Alive. Laughing. Together. Our ice doesn't even have time to melt before we're pouring another drink and telling another story."

The torch shone on his face and she watched as he blinked away a tear. "I'm glad you're happy."

"I'm glad you exist," he admitted. "I know you have to go home. You have a life there. But I hope that we will have some more time together at some point."

"My parents will insist on meeting you. Insist might be too gentle of a word. And they're not patient people. I hope you can come see us soon. My father can't travel much, his back is a problem for him." Her gaze fell down toward the boards of the pier as she thought of her father's pain.

"I'd like that a lot. They've raised a very wonderful girl. I can tell. I'd be happy to go see them but I would like to wait until after my father passes."

"You're going to go see him?"

"I think so. And I want to make sure he's got some proper funeral services too. I called my sisters this afternoon to talk about it all. I've been doing a lot of thinking. I wouldn't want to leave town until after."

"I understand."

"But I do really want to meet them," he assured her.

"You shouldn't ever have to worry about a dull moment once you meet the Fox family."

"Good." Mark patted her knee as he rose. "I think I'll go fill some more glasses."

Griff was back and she knew instantly something was off. His smile wasn't genuine but forced.

"What's wrong?" She asked patting the chair next to her, but he didn't sit.

"You left your phone in the house. It was ringing like crazy. I didn't recognize the number but they just kept calling so I thought maybe it was an emergency."

"Is it my parents?"

"No," he said, his brows coming together as he handed the phone over. "It was Ryan. He had a lot to say."

Her heart moved from one kind of worry to a new one. Her family was safe, but something else was in danger. "He shouldn't have called."

"Well, I don't blame the guy. When you propose to someone you do hope for an answer." Griff looked wounded in a way that broke her heart.

"Griff, he's nuts. I'm not going to marry him."

"Even after that great kiss?"

"It wasn't like that," she stammered. "Please just let me explain."

"Gwen, I already know you don't want to marry Ryan. He knew exactly what he was doing on that phone call and I could see right through him. He sounded desperate. I would be too if I thought I had a shot with you and might lose it."

"He doesn't have a shot with me. I didn't tell you about the kiss or the proposal because they meant nothing to me."

"I know."

"You do?"

"Yes, because I can tell when things mean something to you. I know when you're conflicted or hurting. I know you."

"You do," she said, popping to her feet. "And I know you."

"Tonight is a good night," he said, gesturing down the pier at the rest of the group.

"So are we good?" she asked, lacing her hand in his.

"We're good." He leaned over and kissed the top of her head. It should have flooded her with relief. But she knew Griff wouldn't ruin this night for her. Even if he was hurt or upset, he wouldn't let that overshadow what was happening. He was that good of a guy.

Mark broke into a story about his sisters that captivated everyone. He could barely get the words out between his laughs. Soon she was drawn back into the orbit of the night, pulled away from the nagging worry in her gut. She and Griff were strong. Stronger together. It would be all right.

EPILOGUE

Kerry sat on the edge of her bed and looked down at her suit-case. Tomorrow she'd leave for college. Her flight would be the first she'd ever taken alone. Her mother had offered, maybe even begged a bit, to join her. But Kerry wanted to settle in on her own. It would only be a couple of weeks before her mother would come for a visit. By then Kerry would know her way around and be standing on her own two feet, finally.

As she looked around her room she realized it no longer reflected the reality of her life. It was all photographs from before. Family trips back when no one knew about Gwen. Back when her father lived in the house and her brothers were still talking to them regularly. It was also back when she had friends. Real friends. Trina and Megan were smiling back at her in half the photographs. Their trip to a theme park. Laying out at the beach last summer. They were arm in arm as they walked around the city on a fieldtrip just ten months ago.

None of this existed anymore. She had lost all of it. This room was a shrine to everything she once had. Standing, she moved to the corkboard and began pulling the pins out. These pictures were just memories now. Megan and Trina hadn't spoken a single word to her in six months. Because of them, half the school had iced her out. The other half didn't even know who she was to begin with. When the board was empty she stacked the pictures up and shoved them in her desk drawer. She wasn't worried about the regret that might come from throwing them out. It was the fear that her mother might spot them in the trash and assume, rightly, something was wrong.

Kerry didn't have the energy to explain. She didn't have the time to fall apart. Life was waiting for her in California. A new life. One she could control. There would be no surprise siblings or horrendous ends to lifelong friendships.

Checking her phone again, she went over her list. Everything she needed was packed. There was nothing left to do but wait. She could hear her mother downstairs in the kitchen, banging pots and pans around. Kerry had suggested takeout but her mother insisted on cooking her favorite meal. They'd eat together and Kerry would smile. Smile the way she'd been doing for the last six months. Because that was what her mother needed.

If Kerry needed it, there would be time to cry next week in California where no one was depending on her to be happy. Because it had been a long time since she'd actually been happy and playing the part was exhausting.

Her mother called her down a few minutes later and Kerry caught her reflection in the mirror. She patted down the flyaway strands of hair and worked on her best smile. Her mother needed one more night of this, so she'd give it all she had all the way up until the wheels of the plane lifted off the runway tomorrow. Then she could finally be herself again. She only hoped she remembered how.

ALSO BY DANIELLE STEWART

****

Multi-Author Series including books by Danielle Stewart

All are stand alone reads and can be enjoyed in any order.

Indigo Bay Series:

A multi-author sweet romance series

Sweet Dreams - Stacy Claflin

Sweet Matchmaker - Jean Oram

Sweet Sunrise - Kay Correll

Sweet Illusions - Jeanette Lewis

Sweet Regrets - Jennifer Peel

Sweet Rendezvous - Danielle Stewart

Short Holiday Stories in Indigo Bay:

A multi-author sweet romance series

Sweet Holiday Wishes - Melissa McClone

Sweet Holiday Surprise - Jean Oram

Sweet Holiday Memories - Kay Correll

Sweet Holiday Traditions - Danielle Stewart

BOOKS IN THE BARRINGTON BILLIONAIRE SYNCHRONIZED WORLD

By Danielle Stewart:

Fierce Love

Wild Eyes

Crazy Nights

Loyal Hearts

Untamed Devotion

Stormy Attraction

Foolish Temptations

Surprising Destiny

Lovely Dreams

Perfect Homecoming

You can now download all the Barrington Billionaire books by Danielle Stewart in a "Sweet" version. Enjoy the clean and wholesome version, same story without the spice. If you prefer the hotter version be sure to download the original.

The Sweet version still contains adult situations and relationships.

Fierce Love - Sweet Version

Wild Eyes - Sweet Version

Crazy Nights - Sweet Version

Loyal Hearts - Sweet Version

Untamed Devotion - Sweet Version

Stormy Attraction - Sweet Version

Foolish Temptations - Sweet Version - Coming Soon

FOREIGN EDITIONS

The following books are currently available in foreign translations

German Translation:

Fierce Love

Ungezügelte Leidenschaft

Wild Eyes

Glühend heiße Blicke

Crazy Nights

Nächte, wild und unvergessen

***

French Translation:

Flowers in the Snow

Fleurs Des Neiges

NEWSLETTER SIGN-UP

If you'd like to stay up to date on the latest Danielle Stewart news visit www.authordaniellestewart.com and sign up for my newsletter.

One random newsletter subscriber will be chosen every month this year. The chosen subscriber will receive a $25 eGift Card! Sign up today.

AUTHOR CONTACT INFORMATION

Website: AuthorDanielleStewart.com
Email: AuthorDanielleStewart@Gmail.com
Facebook: facebook.com/AuthorDanielleStewart
Twitter: @DStewartAuthor
Bookbub: https://www.bookbub.com/authors/danielle-stewart
Amazon: https://www.amazon.com/Danielle-Stewart/e/B00CCOYB3O

63719618R00133